TO SAVE A WRETCH

"To Save a Wretch", an adventure novel of the sea with historical undertones, is Roger Lancaster's first novel. He served at sea as a ship's radio officer before marrying Rosemary and settling down as a college lecturer in Bristol, where they brought up their four children.

TO SAVE A WRETCH

Roger Lancaster

58K

fifty eight kings press

First published in Great Britain in 2011 by
fifty eight kings press
3 Mayfield Road, Southam, CV47 0JX

CHAPTER ONE

Ross Clifford could hardly believe he failed to see the warning signs on first meeting John Bridson. Give the man a small moustache and you could have been forgiven for thinking that Adolf Hitler had been resurrected in the form of master of a small merchant vessel here in the nineteen-eighties. Whether Hitler's upper lip ever curled up over yellowing teeth as he spoke, Ross could not be sure, but this should have been a further sign of trouble ahead.

Yet Bridson's first appearance seemed like the answer to all the prayers Ross would have uttered had he been that way inclined.

Sitting out in a cane chair on the ground floor verandah of the hospital in sweltering Freetown, Sierra Leone, still in his dressing-gown, Ross had been wondering how fate could have dealt him such an escalating series of disasters, when nurse Yema, for whose anguished features Ross felt partly responsible, suddenly appeared.

"There's a visitor for you, Ross," she announced dully.

Ross looked up expecting to see the local shipping agent, Mr. Bonema-Jarvis, but he had never seen this man before – a short, thickset European in his mid-fifties, who wore a rumpled beige lightweight suit and carried a large Panama hat, giving Ross the initial impression of a colonial official left behind by the British years ago.

"Mr. Clifford?" the newcomer enquired in a voice which Walt Disney might have given to an irritable cartoon dog.

"Yes."

"Are you feeling better?" growled Ross's visitor.

"Yes, thank you," Ross replied cautiously.

"My name's Bridson. I'm captain of a small general cargo vessel. We're at anchor further down the coast."

Why hadn't Ross seen it immediately? The black Oxford shoes were a dead giveaway. Bridson's fidgeting suggested he would have felt more comfortable wearing the rest of his uniform as well.

"I understand you're a radio officer," Bridson probed, removing the hat and taking a cane chair next to Ross.

"Electronics officer," Ross corrected.

"Sorry. But you can operate and maintain ship's radio communications equipment, can you not?"

"Yes, of course."

"And you're proficient in morse code?"

"Naturally, sir. Satellite communications haven't taken over completely yet."

"My ship is quite elderly, Mr. Clifford. We do have a SATCOM, but I still have a use for the older equipment. The main transmitter and receiver have to be tuned by a skilled person and are keyed in morse. I need an experienced radio officer to operate them."

Ross's face brightened, but he remained cautious.

"I could do that, captain. I've been at sea for ten years, ever since I qualified from college."

"Very good. I can offer you three thousand pounds a month and an ongoing contract into the foreseeable future."

Ross tried hard not to gasp. It was far more money than he had been receiving from the tanker company and they were considered to be among the better payers. Also, it looked as if his old skills learned in his college days would be appreciated, even in these high-tech times. Not least, it was a heaven-sent opportunity to get himself out of his present predicament.

"You have no further commitment to your recent employer?" Captain Bridson had interpreted Ross's silence as hesitation.

"Oh, no," Ross assured him, "I'm due to be shipped back home DBS any day now – not my choice." The initials stood for Distressed British Seaman.

"Then you'll consider my offer?"

"No need to consider, sir. I'll take it."

"Very good!" The captain gave a lip-curling smile over his yellow teeth. "We sail for Charleston, South Carolina, in four day's time."

"And then?"

"Back to Liverpool, from whence we came to this coast."

"Oh." At least it would provide some delay, but Ross's enthusiasm waned at the prospect of returning to the U.K. even after a month or two.

"Something wrong with that?" Bridson's face had fallen.

"No. But… look, sir," Ross struggled for the right words, "I know this may sound a strange request, but… for personal reasons, you understand… I'd rather people – the agent here, for instance – didn't know where I'd gone. You see, sir… "

To Ross's surprise, Captain Bridson's face suddenly lit up.

"Say no more, Mr. Clifford," he beamed. "Half of my ship's company are running away from something or somebody. We don't ask questions of each other. My ship's like the Foreign Legion of the sea."

"Oh. Right. Good."

"Are your wounds healed sufficiently for you to be discharged and to travel?"

"Oh yes, sir. No worries now."

"Very good. Look, we're at anchor in the Sherbro River down south. It's a long drive. Get your kit together and I'll pick you up first thing in the morning – seven o'clock."

"Right, sir."

Captain Bridson replaced his hat and stood, preparing to leave.

"Oh, one more thing, sir," said Ross.

"Yes?"

"What happened to your last radio officer?"

"He jumped ship." The reply was abrupt and accompanied by a fixed glare right into Ross's eyes, followed a second later by another grimacing smile.

4

"Good day, Mr. Clifford. I'll look forward to having you aboard."

After Bridson had gone, Ross slipped his hand beneath his dressing gown to finger the healing scars around his abdomen. He would be all right. He felt fit enough. He couldn't miss this chance. Apart from anything else, three thousand a month was a fortune, even in these inflationary times.

He would be away from Yema, whose beaming smile and raucous laughter had vanished beneath her devastation. Ross knew she did not blame him, but he still felt he had let her down. He had so hoped to repay her care and encouragement by bringing the joy back into her life, but he had failed.

He would avoid the trauma of giving evidence against Geoff back in Britain, at least for a time. Gordon would also be home from America and he might have had to face two bloodthirsty husbands, not to mention Lynette, the woman scorned.

Ross looked out onto the bustling street beyond the hospital yard with a brighter gaze than before. The heat of the afternoon sun suddenly felt less oppressive.

He always enjoyed watching the people walking or cycling past, especially the women in their colourful dresses, their heads bound with what looked like pretty towels. Some carried shopping on the flat tops of their headgear. Most of the men wore simple thin slacks or shorts and tee shirts, but some were clad in brightly-coloured robes – presumably religious leaders of some sort. It may be the poorest country Ross had ever seen, but there were no wars and as long as the people could get sufficient food they seemed content with the simple things in life.

Motor traffic was very light, just the odd poorly-maintained car, van or pick-up. Only once did he see a really large vehicle – a truck carrying a shipping container - which emitted almost human groans as the wheels sank into the deep pot-holes and rose out again.

. . . .

The Land Rover was waiting on time outside the hospital's main entrance.

Bridson still wore his faintly ridiculous suit, hat and black shoes, which contrasted with Ross's thin green tee shirt, beige slacks and flip-flops. The barefoot African driver in khaki shorts and shirt picked up Ross's bags and stowed them in the back and Ross climbed in beside them. Captain Bridson sat in the front with the driver and they set off, bumping through the pot-holed streets and suburbs and onto the main highway to the south.

Ross had left notes for Yema and Mr. Bonema-Jarvis regretting his sudden departure. He assured them he was sufficiently recovered to discharge himself but took care not to give any details of where he was going. The agent would be able to put two and two together, Ross supposed – there would not be many ships around the coast – but he would probably be relieved that Ross was off his hands. Yema would be upset at his leaving without saying anything beforehand, but Ross hated goodbyes at the best of times, and in these circumstances a farewell was too awful to contemplate.

The road was good for the first two hours. Ross tried to make conversation with Captain Bridson, shouting above the noise of the diesel engine.

"What cargo are we carrying?"

"General agricultural produce."

"What's the name of the shipping company?"

"There's no company. The ship's owned by an American – it's the only one he's got."

"Who were you with before?"

"Southern Ocean Lines."

"Wow! Were you captain of one of their cruise liners, then?"

"Yes."

"Didn't you like that life?"

"At times."

It was too much like hard work, so Ross lapsed into silence. For a man to leave the cruise liners of such a prestigious company for a one-ship tramp outfit seemed strange, but Ross sensed it might be a delicate subject with the captain.

He gazed out on the scenery as it rolled by – the wide plains dotted with small dark green trees and carpeted with long brown grasses.

At length they left the main highway and began a much slower drive along a dirt road. The driver had to work hard to avoid craters, his bare feet pummeling the pedals. They crossed a few rivers and streams – some by rickety bridge, others by wooden rafts poled across by skinny men wearing nothing but appallingly grubby shorts. They had to drive through some rivers, with no help at all to hand if they had stuck or stalled in midstream. But the driver seemed to know the way well, taking each little road diversion and each ford crossing with confidence. Or was it bravado?

The heat was beginning to get to Ross. He should have been used to it by now. He loved the really humid tropics of Malaysia and Sri Lanka, provided there was plenty of gin and tonic with ice and lemon to hand, but this was as hot as he could ever remember.

There were people to see most of the journey – just walking along the side of the road. Ross hadn't noticed any places of significance where they could be walking from or to, they just walked, staring straight ahead. Most of the women balanced bundles or pots on their heads, their hips swaying as if to offset any tendency of their loads to tip off such a precarious perch.

Poverty was everywhere, of course, but the locals here in the country looked contented enough, though underfed, just like in Freetown.

Ross's eyelids fluttered. Give these people more food and clean drinking water, air-conditioned huts, fridges, work to do and basic services and it could be a paradise.

One day, when he had made his millions, Ross would return and give them all his money to build up the country and provide them all with a good standard of living. He would show them how to make better use of the fertile land and they would prosper as never before.

He would build a superb road system and modernise the railways. Education would be top class and free to all. The health service would be the best in the world – the Freetown hospital would be transformed into a world centre of medical excellence and Yema would be made Minister of Health. In return the people would honour him, he would be made King Ross the First of Sierra Leone. They would build him a palace and compete to be his servants, some begging to be able to carry him around his realm in a sedan chair, others plying him with exotic food and gins and tonics. Lithe young virgins would camp outside the palace gates, praying to become the next one to be chosen by their beloved leader…

A particularly deep pot-hole jolted Ross upright. His head punched the canvas roof and his eyes shot open in alarm. Bridson and the driver seemed unperturbed.

"Are we nearly there?" Ross enquired, "I could murder a cold lager." His own words prompted a sudden ghastly thought. "It's not a dry ship, is it?"

"Don't worry, Mr. Clifford," Bridson reassured him, "there is every good thing you could want aboard the Duke of Argyll. We should be there in another half-hour."

Funny name for a ship, pondered Ross. Ships should have feminine names, if any gender at all. How could you refer to a ship as 'she' with a name like *Duke of Argyll*?

They began passing through swampland where there were a few villages and some rice paddies, then through palm forests. The air freshened ever so slightly.

It was approaching evening when they pulled up on an isolated river bank at a little jetty where a small launch was moored.

Their driver became the boatman, started the outboard motor and steered them out into the river.

Covering the banks on both sides was an almost unbroken network of tree roots, the branches above keeping the stream near the banks in cool shade. They kept to the unshaded middle, but the sun had lost its intensity now.

They traveled downstream, round a couple of bends and out into a much wider river.

There was the ship, anchored in midstream.

She was even smaller and older than Ross had imagined, no more than three thousand tons, he guessed, not designed for Atlantic crossings. However, she had a sturdy appearance. What looked like the officer accommodation was beneath the bridge, in front of the funnel, with another structure at the stern, presumably cabins for crewmen. The funnel and superstructure were rounded – typical of nineteen-fifties attempts to give a streamlined appearance. The green hull, white upperworks and yellow funnel bore no markings apart from the ship's name and the port of registry on the stern, which Ross could just make out in the gathering dusk: *Duke of Argyll, Monrovia.* The Liberian flag fluttered over the stern.

A barge was tied up on the starboard side and the gangway led down to the waterline on the port side.

Two seamen, Europeans in smart white trousers and shirts, came down the gangway to meet them as the boat pulled alongside. Ross's bags were passed over before Captain Bridson and Ross followed up the steep steps. The boat set off back upstream.

"These are the engineers' quarters," said the captain as they climbed a deck inside the midships accommodation. As they mounted more stairs, he announced the purpose of each deck in turn.

"Dining saloon and wardroom on this deck."

"Most officers, including yourself, on this deck."

They stopped outside the radio officer's cabin and the seamen placed Ross's bags inside before leaving.

"I'm up on the next deck with my chief officer and above that is the bridge and radio office. I'll introduce you to everyone at dinner, which will be in an hour's time."

Dinner could not come too soon for Ross. He had had nothing but a few sandwiches and a can of warm lager all day, provided by Bridson as they travelled.

He looked around his plain little cabin – the usual bunk, drawers, wardrobe, desk and washbasin. There was no air-conditioning. The solitary window looked out over the main deck towards the accommodation aft. Ross opened it to let in some of the evening air then, having surveyed the scene, raised the louvred shutter, leaving him in a restful dimness. A little breeze still entered the cabin through the louvres and he could hear the shrill calls of exotic birds and animals.

He stowed his clothes and belongings, shaved and freshened up at his washbasin, then laid back on his bunk to await mealtime.

He heard footsteps out on deck and someone humming a slightly familiar, old-fashioned tune, the title of which he could not recall. Then he heard the voices of two men.

"Stand by to receive a boat from Shebar, Mister Hamilton."

"Aye-aye, sir."

The first speaker's voice was vaguely familiar, but it was not Captain Bridson.

"'Twill be Mister Tucker with five men."

"Aye-aye, sir."

Shebar. That was an exotic-sounding name. Ross promised himself he would look for it on the chart sometime. He must have dozed off, as the next thing he heard was the beating of a gong. Dinner time at last.

There was just one long table in the small dining saloon. Captain Bridson introduced all the officers to Ross briefly in a blur of names.

They were all in smart uniforms – white shirts with shoulder epaulettes indicating rank, and navy blue trousers – which made Ross feel underdressed, still in his civilian tee shirt and lightweight slacks. He had a similar uniform himself but was seldom required to wear it on his recent ships.

The mate, or chief officer as the captain liked to call him, was Samuel Marshall, a tall thin man in his late forties, who seemed to be putting on an act of being an eccentric, using a monocle to inspect the menu and calling everybody 'Old Boy'. The second mate was Ian Hamilton, a Scot, whose name Ross remembered from the conversation he had overheard on deck, a big fellow of about thirty with a black beard and black, curly hair. There was no third mate, which suggested that the captain would keep one of the bridge watches himself. The other officers present were two engineers, whose names Ross had not been able to take in.

There were empty chairs, but some would be on watch, of course. Then, as the officers finished their soup a new arrival entered the room and approached the table.

Ross regretted a split second later that he had not kept his cool, instead his jaw must have dropped a couple of inches as the tall, beautiful blonde in the white dress reached a vacant chair next to Bridson. The Captain stood up and the other officers followed suit, as did Ross rather belatedly. They all resumed their seats as the girl sat down herself next to the Captain.

On her shoulders, gold and red epaulettes were brushed by her long, blonde hair.

"This is our surgeon, Miss Arthur," the captain announced to Ross. She nodded at Ross.

"Hello," said Ross weakly.

A doctor? On a little ship like this? There was something funny here, but Ross kept his mouth shut. A doctor was not required aboard any ship carrying fewer than a hundred persons on long voyages, and that excluded all ships except cruise liners.

She had blue eyes, full red lips and high cheekbones, reminding Ross of a nineteen-fifties film star. Her dress was modest but could not conceal the fact that an Ursula Andress figure lurked beneath. She was in her mid-twenties, Ross guessed, and there was no need to ask why the Old Man had seated her next to himself.

There was barely any conversation and Ross, remembering the captain's words about not asking questions, tried to concentrate on the food. There was some small talk about the heat and tides and speculation as to a sailing date some days hence. Ross could not help stealing glances at the girl, but her eyes lowered whenever there was any danger of them meeting his.

After dinner, Ross visited his radio office on the bridge deck, just aft of the chart room. The equipment was indeed mixed. It included a SATCOM satellite radiotelephone – the very latest thing - and the old transmitter and receiver the captain had mentioned were also there. A modern lifeboat transmitter sat in a corner – the very latest type which could float and send out distress signals automatically.

He strolled into the chart room, where he spotted the satellite navigation equipment – again the most modern technology – also the weather fax machine, echo sounder and short-range VHF radiotelephone. Then he passed out onto the bridge to view the two radars. He would be responsible for all this equipment.

"The wee radar's not performing as well as it used to." Ross turned to see that Ian Hamilton, the second mate, had walked in behind him.

"Right. I'll check everything out in the morning," Ross replied. "No chance of us sailing for a couple of days, I suppose?"

"Naw. More like four."

"That will give me plenty of time to get everything in good shape."

"The last sparkie let things go a wee bit, mind," warned Ian Hamilton.

"Thanks for the tip. I hear he jumped ship."

"You could say that."

"Where?"

"Och, further up the coast."

"Funny place to jump ship. A girl there, I suppose?"

"Who knows the mind o' some folk?"

Ross wanted to steer the conversation around to what really intrigued him, but seeing no subtle way of doing so, he posed the question directly.

"Why the doctor?"

"Aye, I thought you'd be asking about her. I saw ye ogling her at dinner. Don't let the Old Man hear you calling her a doctor. She's his surgeon. He's from Southern Ocean Lines and he brought the mate with him. They like to run this ship like one of their old liners, where the quack's called a surgeon. Barmy! It's a wonder they dinna have a purser too."

"Is that why you wear uniforms?"

"Aye. White shirt, shorts, socks and shoes in the daytime, Red Sea rig in the evenings. Have ye no got them?"

"I have", Ross affirmed, "though whether they'll still fit me is another matter. What's the doctor's – I mean surgeon's – first name?"

"Bobbie."

"Unusual."

"She's a Yank."

"Oh, right. Is she the Old Man's… you know…?"

"There're plenty o' rumours, especially on a wee ship like the Duke." Ian Hamilton certainly knew how to be non-committal. Perhaps he himself was… "Hmm. Right. I'll go and turn in, then," said Ross, keeping his thoughts to himself, "it's been a long day. I'll make an early start in the morning."

"Aye. Breakfast's at eight."

"Right. You'll be watching for your boat, then."

"What boat?"

"The one from – where was it? – Shebar?"

"I dinna ken of any boat."

"Oh, I thought I heard you on deck before dinner talking about a boat being due."

"Naw. Not me."

The look he received from the second mate seemed to be querying Ross's sanity.

Ross shrugged his shoulders.

"Must have misheard," he said feebly. "See you tomorrow, then. Good night."

"G'night."

Back in his cabin, Ross sat on his bunk. Through the louvred shutter over the open window he heard footsteps, like someone pacing slowly up and down, then a man's voice.

"Mary! Oh, Mary!" Ross heard. "I see thy beauty reflected from yonder pole star. God be with thee, my sweet Mary."

Amateur dramatics? Ross wondered. It was the same voice he had heard before. Where *had* he heard that voice previously?

A silence followed, the footsteps ceased. Then the man's voice began singing softly. It was the same tune Ross had heard him humming outside before dinner, but this time the words were sung. It was a hymn.

*"**How sweet the name of Jesus sounds in a believer's ear**,"* went the song. *"**It soothes his sorrows, heals his wounds, and drives away his fear.**"*

God! thought Ross. What kind of ship was this that he had come to?

Cautiously, silently, he lowered the shutter to peer out. The singing had stopped. It took a few moments for his eyes to become accustomed to the dimly lit deck. At first he could see no-one there, just the covered hatch and two ventilator cowls.

Then he spotted the white dress and long, blonde hair fluttering gently in the breeze by the ship's rail. She was gazing out into the blackness across the river. Ross's tongue moved slowly across his dry lips. Suddenly, she turned and walked back towards the accommodation from where Ross was looking out. The clip-clip of her high heels was not the same sound as the footsteps he had heard earlier.

A minute later he heard the same clip-clip on the stairs and in the alleyway outside his cabin. Then a door opened and closed.

After a minute or so, Ross ventured out into the alleyway. He studied the nameplates above each door. The one next to his cabin said "SECOND OFFICER" and one further down on the other side of the alleyway denoted "SURGEON". The surgeon's nameplate was new. The cabin had probably been for a third mate originally.

He returned to his own cabin, dug out his old uniforms and tried them on. Luckily they still fitted, if a little tighter than he remembered. Then he undressed, and climbed into bed.

"Bobbie," he said softly as his head touched the pillow. Then he slept.

CHAPTER TWO

Neither Captain Bridson nor his surgeon were at breakfast. Having a long lie-in, no doubt. A bitter scowl crossed Ross's features. How could a girl like that… ? Okay, he was the captain. But Bridson! Old enough to be her father – grandfather even.

Ross jabbed his spoon into his boiled egg so forcefully that it penetrated the shell at the bottom.

He turned his attention to the mate, in order to break the silence as much as anything else.

"You were with Southern Ocean Lines, I hear," he said.

"That's right, old boy."

"Were you mate there?"

"Chief Officer. Yes. Rather."

"Did you sail with Captain Bridson there too?"

"Yes. On several occasions, actually."

"You must find this ship a bit of a comedown after a cruise liner, don't you?"

Ross felt a kick under the table and received a warning glare from Ian Hamilton.

"There are compensations, old bean," said the mate. He hurriedly finished his toast and left.

"Tactless, right?" He knew it had been, but Ross was in no mood to be sensitive to the feelings of others.

"Their ship ran aground in Nassau harbour with nine hundred passengers aboard," Ian explained.

"Oh, I remember reading about that," nodded Ross, then grinned. "So it was them, was it?"

"They were both blamed and given the sack. A mite unfairly, from my understanding of the incident."

"Scapegoats, eh?"

"Aye."

"Are either of them religious?"

Ian almost choked on his toast.

"No," he said emphatically after he had recovered, "definitely not."

"Is there anybody on board who would sing a hymn?"

"Why? D'ye want to start a choir?"

"No. It's just that I heard someone singing a hymn on deck last night. It sounded out of place, somehow."

"Aye, it would do. I don't know of anyone into hymn-singing aboard this ship."

The Scot was eyeing Ross with some suspicion. It was the second time Ross had mentioned hearing voices on deck to Ian. But he had heard it, so why shouldn't he say so? Ross shrugged his shoulders to end that topic of conversation.

After breakfast, Ross began checking all the equipment under his control. He re-tuned the radars to improve their range, then tested the gear in the radio office, where Captain Bridson paid him a visit, handing him a sheet of paper with details of a radio station typed on it.

"I shall have messages for this station from time to time. Watch out on these channels every day, even in port, to see if there's any message for us. All the times and frequencies are there."

"Right, sir."

Ross studied the details after the captain had gone. No name was given to the station, only the call letters – WCH. The W indicated that it was in the U.S.A. The frequencies meant he would have to use the big transmitter and morse code. He searched the book of call letters but there was no listing for any WCH.

Ross frowned. The last radio officer must have failed to update the books.

All the equipment worked well, so Ross walked out onto the bridge wing to see what was going on.

One of the ship's cranes was lifting a large wooden crate from the barge alongside. Groaning noises implied a very heavy load, straining the cables. The crane coped, however, and swung the box over the open hatch, then lowered it into the depths of the hold.

Ross looked at his watch. It was time to listen in to the radio station the captain had told him about. He returned to the radio office. Switching on the receiver and donning the headphones, he tuned around for WCH. There it was, sending out a call in morse to ELIW, the call letters of the *Duke of Argyll*. Ross switched on the big transmitter and adjusted the tuning. He really should not have been using transmitters in port, but he doubted whether anybody would ever notice in this place. WCH replied quickly to his call and began sending the message.   It was all in code, five-digit groups of mixed letters and figures, meaningless to Ross, but not uncommon.   Shipping companies often had their own codes to prevent their competitors discovering their trading practices.

He typed it onto a message form as he received it and tapped out an acknowledgement on the morse key after it had ended.

He switched off the equipment, sealed the message in an envelope and set off to look for the captain.

The Old Man's cabin was locked and there was no response to Ross's knocking. The mate's cabin was open and empty, as was Ian's. Ross hovered near the surgeon's door, but not for too long. He had a good excuse. He knocked.

"Yes?" It was her voice.

Ross entered to find her sitting at her desk, operating a computer – not something normally seen on any ship. It was the very latest kind too - green screen, keyboard, twin disk drives all in one big case. The cabin was slightly larger than Ross's and with a better outlook – forward over number one hatch, the foredeck and bows – but the room was crammed with medical books, which left little space for anything else.

Her long hair swept round like a curtain of gold as she turned to face him.

Ross gave her what he considered to be a rugged smile. A girl had once told him he looked like Rock Hudson.

"Hello. I was looking for the captain. A message for him."

"Not he-ah, as you can see." Her southern accent was very appealing.

"Right. Sorry. You wouldn't know where he is, I suppose?"

"He could be anywhe-ah around the ship. Jack likes to do a daily inspection of the whole vessel, just like on his old cruise boats."

"Right. I'll go and look for him, then. Thanks."

"Good hunting."

Was she making fun of him? Ross wondered as she fluttered her long eyelashes, giving only the slightest hint of a smile. Ross backed out and closed the door.

Jack, she had called him. Ross had not heard anyone else refer to the captain by his first name, not even the mate. Ross descended a deck and checked the wardroom and dining saloon, then another deck to try the engineers' cabins.

A further deck down he opened the big steel door which led down to the engine-room and surveyed the scene. He noted the huge diesel main engine and the smaller auxiliary generator, which produced the electricity when the main engine was shut down, as now. Nothing could have been done to update the ship here since she had been built.

The second engineer was mounting the steel companionway towards Ross. He confirmed the captain was not there.

Ross turned back. There were only a few storerooms here, but the alleyway led to the sheltered walkways leading aft along both sides of the ship. Ross followed one, passing a heavy steel door leading to number two hold, and kept going until he reached the crew quarters aft.

He recognized one of the stewards and one of the seamen who had carried his bags aboard, but the captain was not here either.

Returning forward on the other side of the ship, Ross finally spotted Captain Bridson at the top of the gangway, talking to an African. The visitor descended the gangway as Ross approached.

"Message for you, sir," Ross announced.

He waited while the Old Man read the form in case there was a reply.

"This is three days old," snapped Captain Bridson angrily.

"It was the first chance I had to get it," Ross explained.

The captain scowled at the perfectly valid reason for the delay.

"No reply," he said. "You'll make sure not to miss any of these schedules with WCH, will you not?"

"Right, sir."

Ross spent the afternoon doing paper work in his radio office. He tuned in to WCH again but there was no call this time.

After dinner, he was lying on his bunk when he heard people out on deck. There were more of them this time, quite a lot of movement.

"Mister Marshall, take the longboat with three gentlemen across to Mister Tucker at daybreak, if you please. He has promised me some trade."

"Aye-aye, sir."

"Mister Tucker's the only one I trust here. The rest be villains all."

Ross had definitely heard that voice before, and it was not aboard this ship.

"Mister Bridson, take the yawl down to Kittam at first light. The King of Charra has gone before to look for trade for me. Have four gentlemen accompany you."

"Very good, sir."

Captain Bridson calling somebody else sir? Could the owner himself be aboard? It wasn't an American accent.

"You may both stand down until the morrow. Mister Hamilton will keep the night watch."

The pub in Liverpool! That's where Ross had heard that voice before. He knew it! That old-fashioned way of speaking he had never heard anywhere else.

. . . .

Having escaped the clutches of the beautiful, scheming Lynette, he had made for Liverpool to secure a berth on the first available tanker heading as far away as possible. The tanker company's office was closed by the time he got there, so he had an evening and a night to kill.

An old waterfront bar, just beyond the reach of the spreading new concrete city centre and saved only by a preservation order served after years of campaigning, was the venue Ross chose for his evening meal.

As he sipped his pint of Newcastle brown and picked at a sandwich, he glanced around at the clientele. Students mostly, he assumed. Certainly there wasn't a seaman amongst them.

He wished he could be transported back in time to the days when the place had been filled with seafaring men. He had never known anything like that, of course. The few modern seamen who remained were professional technical people like himself – not the type to hang around yarning in dockside bars.

Then, as if deliberately to confound his thoughts, he began overhearing two men talking at a table behind him. He did not turn round for fear of revealing his interest and inhibiting their conversation. They sounded very senior from the old-fashioned way they spoke, one with a grossly exaggerated north country dialect. Ross did not recognize the other accent.

"I need th' services again, John. Th'll be prepared to take command now, will th'?"

"Aye. You honour me greatly, Mister Manesty, to trust me as master of one of your famous fleet. Though I'm grieved at having to leave my beloved new wife."

"Ah! Mary. What a fortunate man, th' be, John."

"Blessed, sir. Naught less."

"But th'll be requiring an enhanced salary with th' new commitments, and a new shipment is urgently needed in Antigua.   The snow's waiting down at the pierhead now."

Snow? Wasn't that slang for heroin – or cocaine? Ross clutched the handle of his glass.

"Aye.   I've seen the vessel.   She's very old. Scarcely fit to lie in a dock or make a Gravesend voyage."

"Do not judge by appearances, John - she's far better found than the Greyhound."

"She'd need to be." The words were spoken with an audible shudder.   "I've no wish to repeat that experience, sir."

"Neither th' will, John. Old she may be, but she's proved herself many a long voyage.   So what dost th' say?"

"The Antigua run, you said?"

"That's right."

"Ye've been a great benefactor to me, Mister Manesty. I accept, and am indeed honoured."

Ross listened for more but there was only silence – not even the clink of glasses to seal the apparent agreement. He shifted his chair and his position in it so that he could view surreptitiously the table behind him.

The two chairs had been vacated and two empty pewter beer mugs had been left on the table. He could see only young people – students, or single people at least – some playing darts.   Then he just caught sight of a door closing behind someone at the far end of the room. All he saw of the person was a man's lower leg, wearing a boot, and a dark coat reaching to calf-length.

. . . .

27

This was definitely the same voice – so distinctive. The man called John.

Ross lowered the shutter at his window and peered out, but all had gone quiet again and no-one was to be seen on deck.

There was a knock at his cabin door.

"Come in," he called.

It was Ian Hamilton.

"D'ye fancy a wee dram in the wardroom?"

"Right!" Ross jumped eagerly off his bunk. So many of his recent ships – the tankers – had been 'dry', so this was a definite plus for the *Duke of Argyll*.

The wardroom was small, even smaller than the dining saloon, with two tables, a few chairs, a tiny self-service bar and a small library in a glass-fronted cabinet.

"Scotch?" asked Ian as if there was nothing else available.

"Fine."

Ian poured the very large drinks, added ice, signed a bar chit and returned to Ross.

"There's a wee deck just out there," he said, motioning to a side door.

It was a little verandah deck, a mere balcony, overlooking the ship's side. They sat in two rattan chairs by a small matching table. The river and the wooded banks beyond could not be seen through the darkness but they could be sensed in the balmy air of the tropical evening. Chirrupping and squawking sounds of the wildlife floated across the water. It was very pleasant.

"Cheers," they said together.

Ross chose his words carefully, not wishing to reveal he had heard more voices out on deck.

"Do you ever have the owner visit his ship?"

"Naw. We never see him. He's a Yank."

The fact seemed to explain many things to Ian.

"Would he be any relation to our doctor – sorry, surgeon?"

"I wouldn't know. Never thought of it myself. But now you mention it, it might explain a few things."

"You mean why she's here at all?"

Ian shrugged.

"I thought she'd be the Old Man's girlfriend."

"Naw. Definitely not."

"Are you sure? She calls him Jack."

"So do most of us behind his back."

"The mate, then?"

Ian laughed.

"Even less likely."

"Not you?"

"Naw. I've a dear wife and four bonny bairns at home."

"Is your wife's name Mary?" Ross instantly regretted blurting out the question.

"Naw. Linda. Why d'ye think it's Mary?"

"Oh, just a guess," Ross replied lamely under Ian's quizzical glare. "Are you telling me the only woman on board has no boy friend? One of the engineers, perhaps?"

"I don't think so. Some of them have tried it on, mind, but got nowhere. They've a nickname for her – a mite unkind."

"What's that?"

"The virgin surgeon. Not the sort of phrase a boy friend would use, eh? So if you fancy your chances, I'd say ye've got a clear field."

"Hmm."

"Another wee dram?"

"Not for me. But don't let me stop you." Ross didn't want to be drunk in the event of the surgeon appearing.

Ian fetched himself another large scotch and they told each other their career stories.

Ian had been made redundant twice and spent long stretches out of work. With a wife and four children and knowing no other occupation than the sea, he had had a hard time. He spoke as if trying to justify his presence aboard the *Duke*, yet there was no need. He was earning a high salary and his job now seemed as secure as any. Why shouldn't he be here? He refilled his glass five or six times during their conversations, but Ross declined each invitation to take more himself.

Then Ross spotted the girl down on deck, leaning over the rail, looking out across the water, just as she had done the night before, her hair glinting beneath the deck lighting..

"Look, Ian. Isn't she gorgeous?"

By this time Ian's speech was slurred, his Scottish accent becoming even more pronounced, his eyelids repeatedly closing and darting open again.

"Aye. The last sparkie thought so too."

"Really? Did he… you know… ?"

"Och, I doubt it. But he was keen all right. If he did get anywhere, it didn't do him much good."

"Why do you say that?"

"Disappeared, ye ken. Over the wall."

"I thought he jumped ship further up the coast. To be with a girl ashore, didn't you say?"

"You said that, not me. Naw. It was at sea. One morning he didna appear. We searched the ship. Not a sign of him. Everything normal in his cabin. No clues anywhere."

"What? D'you think it was something to do with his interest in her then?"

"I dinna ken. I keep m'sel' to m'sel'."

Just then the girl turned and walked back towards the accommodation.

Ross leapt to his feet while Ian continued to ramble.

"Naw, I ken it was just this ship. It gets to ye. O' course ye know what Bridson and Marshall are up to, don't you?"

"Not right now, Ian," said Ross as he made a move to leave. "I think I'll turn in. See you in the morning."

"Aye. Okay. Don't go disappearing now, will ye? We don' want that all over again. Naw, we don' want that."

But Ross did not hear. He was already leaving the wardroom.

He waited at the top of the stairs from the deck below, expecting any second to hear the clip-clip of high-heeled shoes.

He waited, but there was no sound on the stairs.

At last he descended to the engineers' deck. There was no sign of anyone. He listened outside each engineer's cabin door but heard nothing anywhere.

Down to the deck below, he looked aft towards the crew quarters – nothing. He crossed to the other side – nothing there either. He opened the door to the engine-room – the third was down there on his own.

He closed the door and returned upstairs to his own cabin.

She must have gone to somebody's cabin. Perhaps to an engineer's, or even down to the sailors' and stewards' quarters aft.

He lowered the shutter and looked out on deck. There was no-one there. He raised it again. How could she just disappear?

Perhaps she had walked forward on the main deck instead of entering the accommodation. He ran up to the bridge and gazed out across the foredeck towards the bow. The decks were fully lit but no-one was there either.

Bobbie Arthur, where are you? he shouted inside his brain.

He looked at his watch. It was after eleven.

On his way back to his cabin, he paused outside the captain's cabin and listened. Nothing.

32

He heard someone mounting the stairs below, but it was not what he wanted to hear – it was a heavy shuffling sound.

Ross half descended the stairway towards the officers' deck to see Ian steering a wandering course to his cabin. Ian fumbled at the cabin door and opened it, giving a loud belch. He entered and slammed the door shut. Ross heard a dull thud and a Scottish curse.

Ross returned once more to his own cabin and laid back on his bunk.

He closed his eyes for a few seconds.

"Mister Arthur!"

The shout from outside Ross's window startled him. *Mister* Arthur?

"Cap'n Newton, sir?" It was undoubtedly a man's voice.

"Has Mister Corrigall prepared the men's room to your satisfaction?"

"There is still some work left to be done, sir."

"Is there space for another ten?"

"Yes, sir. Perchance fifteen."

"Very well. Please exhort Mister Corrigall to complete the work by Friday noon. We sail for the Plantains on the afternoon tide."

Ross resisted the temptation to lower the window shutter. Something told him that those out on deck might not welcome an eavesdropper.

Mister Arthur? Was the surgeon's father on board? Or husband? She wore no ring. Surely somebody would have said. The other names – Newton and Corrigall – he had not heard before.   The man addressed as Newton, though, was the one whose voice he recognized from the Liverpool pub.   And *Captain* Newton? Could there be *two* captains aboard?

As for sailing for the Plantains – what or where was that? Some tiny port near Charleston, perhaps?

Ian had been about to tell him something just before he had shot off to try and intercept the surgeon. What had he said?   Something about what Bridson and Marshall were up to…

The silence outside was broken, this time by the voice belonging to the man called Newton.   It was the same voice that had spoken of a girl called Mary and had sung the verse of a hymn.   Whoever this Newton was, he was singing a hymn again…

> *"Thou art coming to a king;*
> *Large petitions will thee bring;*
> *For his grace and power are such*
> *None can ever ask too much."*

Another mention of a king.   Which king's name had been mentioned before?   Charra, or something like that.   Some local tribal chief, by the sound of it.   Ian might know.   He would have to get Ian on the scotch again and find out what was really going on.   Meanwhile, the hymn continued…

> *"While I am a pilgrim here,*
> *Let thy love my spirit clear;*
> *Be my guide, my guard, my friend,*
> *Lead me to my journey's end."*

That seemed to be the end of the song, too.

Ross heard footsteps on the deck. They were receding.

He sprang from the bunk to the window and released the shutter, letting it fall with a crash.

There was nothing to be seen, the deck completely deserted.

Too slow.

Or was he imagining it all? Surely not. Yet it was all such nonsense, like a fanciful dream remembered.

As he pulled up the shutter again, he noticed that the palms of his hands were running with sweat. In spite of the warm, tropical evening, the perspiration sticking his shirt to his back was cold.

He would have to talk to someone about it. Perhaps he could confide in Ian. At least if there was a logical explanation, Ian might be able to supply it, although he was reluctant to admit to hearing voices a third time to the second mate.

If he was indeed imagining it all, he needed professional advice. From a doctor.

Of course!

He sat back on his bunk, struggling to weigh the pros and cons of what was crossing his mind.

It would not be the best of chat-up lines. It might even ruin his chances with her forever.

Yet it would be original…

CHAPTER THREE

It was eleven the next morning by the time Ross managed to pluck up enough courage to go and knock on the surgeon's door.

"Come in." She was there!

Ross opened the door. She turned elegantly away from her computer screen to look at him. Her white dress had buttons all the way down the front and the lower ones were undone, allowing Ross a glimpse of her shapely white-stockinged legs.

"Yes?" she queried.

"Hello. I wonder if I might have a word with you. In your professional capacity."

"Oh. Sure. Come on in."

She indicated that he should sit on the bunk. It was the only place left for him to sit anyway, no doubt doubling as a doctor's couch during the day when she was not gracing it herself. There would not be any doctor's surgery on a ship as small as this. Ross sat on it reverently, wondering what she would wear when she retired to bed.

"What's the trouble?"

"Well, you know I had operations recently."

"Yes, ah heard. A knife attack, wasn't it?"

"Right."

"Nasty. What did you do to deserve that?"

"Oh, just a misunderstanding with the third engineer. His wife was on board and, er, he thought I was, er ... "

"Okay," she said, holding up a hand, "I didn't mean to pry. But you recovered all right, I was told."

"Yes, I think so."

"You're not sure?"

"Not entirely."

"You want me to check you over?"

"That might not be necessary..."

"Mebbe I should anyway."

"Should you?"

"Sure. Let's see the scars."

Perhaps it was necessary to justify his ploy to talk with her. Ross undid his shorts and lowered them partially, lifting his shirt to reveal the scars.

She laid her delicate, creamy-white fingers with their red-painted nails gently across the scars and peered at them very closely. Her long, blonde hair hung forward, brushing lightly against him. He could feel her breath on him. Modest as her dress was, from this angle he could see something of what lurked beneath the top button. She must have sensed - or seen - Ross's reaction, as she straightened up and backed away. Ross thought he caught the faintest signs of a blush across her normally serene face.

"That would seem to have healed real good, er... Ross, isn't it?"

"Yes, Miss Arthur."

"Bobbie. Everybody calls me Bobbie."

Among other things, thought Ross.

"That's unusual."

"Not so much where I come from," Bobbie

smiled. "Does everything feel okay."

"Perfectly normal." Ross was anxious to assure her. "Never better."

"So why come to me? Is there anything else on your mind?"

He couldn't tell her that, could he. Not yet, anyway.

."Well..... do you think it's possible that I could have sustained any slight brain damage? Perhaps from the anaesthetics they use in this country?"

"What makes you think that?"

Ross hesitated, but he had gone too far to back down now.

"I've been hearing voices."

"Voices? In your head?"

"They seem to be coming from out on deck at night, but when I look out of my window there's nobody there."

She frowned. He had been right, it was not a good chat-up line.

"What do the voices say?"

"Seamen's talk, but speaking in an old-fashioned way. And singing hymns."

Ross had expected some sort of reaction - perhaps a sympathetic assurance that he was under stress and just needed time to get over his recent ordeal, but her response was quite different.

"Has anyone been talking to you about Owen?" she asked.

"Who?"

"Owen Kavanagh."

"Who's he?"

"The previous radio officer."

"What's he got to do with it?"

"He said he heard the same sort of things."

"Oh, thank God!" said Ross, sitting back heavily on the bunk. "I'm not going mad after all." He realised she was staring at him and his grin evaporated. "Oh, I see. He *did* go mad, didn't he. Over the wall."

"I thought you said nobody told you about Owen?"

"Well, not by name. Ian told me the last radio officer had disappeared, presumably over the side."

"That's all?"

"Yes."

"And nobody's mentioned to you that he told several people he'd heard these voices?"

"No. It might have made more sense to me if they had."

"The others thought he was crazy. He sure was disturbed. I gave him mild sedatives. If what you say is true - that you haven't heard of Owen's problems before, I mean..."

"No. Definitely not."

"Hmm. I should have taken Owen more seriously. He was a nice guy. He only joined us in Liverpool."

"Liverpool! That's where I first heard the voices. In a pub."

"But that must have been before the attack on you."

"Yes."

"Look, Ross, if this is psychological, it's beyond my experience. But if both yourself and Owen heard these voices, mebbe somebody else could too. Next time you hear them, seek me out. I'll come along and see if I can hear anything."

Ross sat upright. Things were suddenly getting better.

"Right."

"If I'm not around, perhaps Ian... "

"No, I don't think so. I've already dropped hints to Ian and he would only say I was barking mad. Now that I've told you, and you believe me, can we just keep it between ourselves for the time being?"

"Sure."

"Great. I expect it's some member of the crew trying to play tricks. I've known people before - shipmates who seemed perfectly normal - get up to some weird games after they've been at sea for a while."

"Sure. Small closed groups - not the healthiest of situations. But if somebody is doing this, he needs to be stopped. He could already be responsible for one suicide."

"Right. Between us we could clear it up." He rubbed his hands together and stood, preparing to leave.

Bobbie rose also. Because of the compactness of the cluttered cabin, they were forced to stand very close.

"Thanks," said Ross. "I'm glad I came to you."

"Y'all take care now," she purred - encouragingly, as Ross thought.

He ached to take her in his arms and plant a kiss on those sensual lips, but this wasn't the right occasion. As he left, she returned to her computer.

Ross stepped out of the cabin, closing the door behind him. He ran down the stairs and out onto the hot steel deck, breathing in great gulps of air.

He crossed to the ship's side and gripped the top rail tightly, not even noticing the burning heat from it.

After he had calmed down, he went up to the wardroom, poured himself a stiff gin and tonic, and sat out on the verandah, gazing across the brown river towards the densely-wooded bank.

What on earth were people doing behind that curtain of dense vegetation?

. . . .

Four fine young men, credits to their tribe - Tamba, Baki, Kothong and Mani - emerged from different directions to the edge of the oil palm plantation where they had been working all morning and laid down their machetes.

Baki spread out the square plastic sheet on the grass and pulled it tight while Mani carefully placed a machete in each corner to hold it down.

The four sat around the sheet, one on each side, and produced lunch packets, bottles of water and spinning tops from the small bags they carried.

After their brief meal they began the serious business of the top spinning contest.

Kothong was usually the winner - his top was finely balanced and his strong fingers set it whining its

41

way onto the sheet where it hummed for counts of up to twenty, or even more, before finally toppling. But Tamba was not far behind - he had spent some hours polishing his top and he felt that today he might just get the better of Kothong.

Suddenly, Baki raised a hand and stared into the rows of oil palms, cocking an ear.

"What?" asked Mani.

"I thought I heard someone in there," he said.

The four peered into the rows, straining to see beyond the point where the brown trunks merged into blackness.

Baki shrugged his shoulders and they returned to the game. Mani made one of his best throws and won some applause from the others.

They all turned sharply at the unmistakable sound of a footfall in the ferns. Kothong cried out and they all froze in disbelief as four men dressed in scruffy khaki and carrying guns stepped out from behind tree trunks and approached them menacingly.

Tamba had heard the stories of the war across the border in Liberia and there had been incursions but no incidents or sightings within fifty miles. How had they managed to penetrate so far west? He eyed the nearest machete, which was within his reach, but he would not have stood a chance. The guns were pointing straight at them and one of the raiders at least had spotted the knives. He approached under the cover provided by his companions and gathered up their only hopes of retaliation, wrapping them in a piece of sacking.

Another paramilitary motioned them to stand and their hands were roughly tied behind their backs. With a shove from behind, they were marched off to the dirt road where a small truck was parked. They were bundled over the tailboard and lashed to the sides while their captors climbed on and they set off southwards.

As the truck bounced its way along the road, Tamba found himself staring at one of the gunmen. He had seen him somewhere before, he felt sure - in one of the neighbouring villages, he thought. Tamba had never knowingly seen a terrorist before.

After about ten miles, the truck turned off into the bush and about fifteen minutes later came to a stop. Two of the captors got down and pulled at a tall pile of cut dead branches. A great steel door was revealed, which they unlocked and pulled open. The four farm workers were ordered into a steel prison. There were only a few small gratings at the tops of the walls near the ceiling, which did not allow much light inside because of all the undergrowth almost covering the box, but there was enough for them to see others inside, manacled to angle-iron on the walls. The four were similarly clamped and their captors went outside.

One of them returned with the sack-covered machetes and placed the package alongside Tamba, tucking it between Tamba's bottom and the wall. He raised his index finger to his lips to recommend silence and Tamba could have sworn he winked before going back outside.

Then the door was slammed to and locked, leaving

them in near darkness.

. . . .

Two purple-black women in their early twenties, wearing floral dresses and headscarves, ambled barefoot down the dirt track. The fishing nets they carried had large wooden hoops at their open end, which were slung over the girls' fine shoulders, while the narrower closed ends of the nets brushed against their pretty calves as they walked.

They giggled as they revealed secrets of their menfolk to each other - extremely intimate details, the sharing of which, had they known, would have caused the males concerned to explode with rage. That was half the fun of telling.

Boi and Mahen were cousins, but were as close as sisters. Their skills at providing fish for their family commune meant that they spent many hours of every day together on the river bank. They had identical tastes in stories, jokes, clothes and almost anything else you could name. They shared everything - except their husbands, of course.

The chattering had to stop as they arrived at the river. Separating themselves by a few yards, they dipped the hoops of their nets into the gently-flowing water and began to concentrate on the art of enticing the suspicious, quivering swimmers through the hoops.

It was only ten minutes later that Mahen snatched her hoop out of the water with a whoosh. A fair-sized fish wriggled in the bottom of the net as she swung it over the bank and down onto the red earth.

She let out a startled cry as a large black bare foot stamped on the net before her eyes. She looked up into the barrel of a gun, above which a man dressed in scruffy, semi-military khakis, grinned down at her.

Turning to Boi, she was dismayed to see her cousin in a similar situation. Another three pseudo-military men stood farther back, looking around into the bush to see if they had been observed.

Obeying the gestures the men made with their guns, the two women were led into the trees in opposite directions.

There were no soldiers posted in this area, Mahen knew. They were probably foreign invaders from Liberia, yet she thought she had seen one of them before. Yes, he was from a neighbouring village, she was sure.

A scream from Boi tore Mahen from her attempts at recognition. She turned to peer into the trees. She saw Boi's clothing strewn around in the ferns. She heard the men shouting excitedly and knew they were doing what everyone had said these sort always did.

The other two advanced on Mahen. She closed her eyes and remained resolutely motionless throughout her ordeal.

At the end of it, the girls were allowed to replace their soiled underclothes and dresses - only their headscarves had not been touched - then their wrists were bound behind their backs. They were too numbed to cry.

As they were marched down the track, Mahen remembered with growing apprehension stories they had heard recently of people disappearing - men as well as women and always young. But most incidents had all happened far to the east, close to the Liberian border, not anywhere near here, only a few miles from the sea.

Mahen saw the same terror in Boi's eyes that she felt inside herself as they eventually came to a small truck and were pushed into the back of it. It was still only mid-morning, it would be some six hours yet before the men of the village even realised they were late getting home.

The truck set off southwards, each minute taking them farther away from their village.

. . . .

Ross visited the radio office to check there was no message from WCH, then returned to the wardroom verandah where he relaxed with another gin and tonic. He had nothing to do now until the next WCH schedule in six hours' time. This was the life!

He gazed out idly at the Sherbro River and beyond. When he became king he would turn this muddy river and its overgrown banks into a superb yachting marina, where billionaires from all over the world would come to spend their fortunes and make his kingdom and its people the most wealthy on earth. Gambling casinos would flourish. He would host the America's Cup race and the place – he would rename it Cliffordville – would be the start and finish of the richest round-the-world yacht race ever staged.

He was not hungry and it was stiflingly hot, so it was an easy decision to skip lunch and have a few more gins.

Peering through his bubbly drink, with its beautiful blue bloom, he visualized the scene as he saw himself transported down the river aboard the royal barge with Queen Bobbie at his side, while the Royal Sierra Leone Air Force conducted a fly-past and air display which would put the Red Arrows to shame.

Finally, he staggered back to his cabin and flopped onto the bunk, where he slept the sleep of the near-enough just.

He failed to hear the light tap at his door or waken to see it open and the surgeon enter quietly. Even though the door was a couple of paces from the bunk, her pretty nose wrinkled at the whiff of Ross's gin-breath. Seeing his collapsed state, she rolled her big beautiful blue eyes upwards before tip-toeing out again.

There were voices to be heard outside Ross's window, but he was oblivious to them.

. . . .

"Inebriated?! At this hour of the day?"

Captain John Newton, master of the snow *Duke of Argyle*, slaver out of Liverpool, his face world-worn beyond his twenty-five years, thundered the words at his first mate, John Bridson. Despite the heat, he wore, as always on deck, the long blue cloak of his rank, which reached down to calf length, black boots and navy blue tricorn hat with its white beading. He strode to the ship's side and slapped the palms of his hands down hard on the massive oak beam before looking over it to the Sherbro

River beneath. He scowled at the three men slumped across the thwarts of the longboat, unable to clamber back aboard unassisted.

"Where did they get the flip at this hour of the day?" he demanded of Bridson.

"The French schooner, sir. They've been carousing aboard her all morning."

"Curse their hides!" bellowed Newton. "They were sent to bring back some trade from the King of Charra. I'll wager those Frenchies have robbed me of it. Clap them in the brig and keep them from the other gentlemen."

"Aye-aye, sir."

"And when you've done that, have the bo's'n arrange for the sails to be loosed and aired."

"Aye-aye, sir."

Newton frowned as the mate set off to carry out his orders. He had to exercise his authority but he could not afford any more trouble. It was only too easy here on the coast for men to desert to another ship or to join the freelance people-catchers ashore. Even mutiny was a possibility with no ship of the Royal Navy in sight.

He raised his spyglass to glower at the French schooner further downstream. He knew that if they could foment unrest among his crew they might be able to poach some if not all of the trade he had painstakingly bargained for.

As Bridson's men secured the longboat and manhandled the drunkards below decks, Newton's glass spotted the shallop returning. As it drew near, he recognized the mulatto Bonema-Jarvis, who had with him five fine-looking man slaves, two women and a boy of about three feet, six inches. This was a more welcome sight, but there was still much space to fill before they could set sail for Antigua. It was not going to be easy.

The ship's surgeon, Robert Arthur, approached the captain.

"Good day, Robert," greeted Newton, always pleased to speak with the one man aboard who he felt was his intellectual and spiritual equal.

The surgeon's face was grim, however.

"Good afternoon, captain. Bad news, I fear, sir. Another man slave succumbed to the flux."

"And the others?"

"Not responding to any treatments, sir."

"Well, you've done your best, Robert. They're all in God's hands now, like the rest of us miserable sinners."

"Aye, sir."

"Get the corpse ready for burial within the hour. And be sure to protect yourself as best you can."

"Aye-aye, sir."

Newton sighed as the surgeon shuffled off to attend to the awful business.

"Hitherto hath the Lord helped us," he muttered to himself.

Such dangers he and his men faced daily, he pondered. Such hard work it all was. How he longed to be back in Chatham with his beloved Mary, perhaps to seek a less demanding position ashore. Yet he knew this was the life the Lord had ordained for him, for the present at least.

The poor wretches he transported to the sugar plantations to the west would undoubtedly stand a better chance of coming to know the Lord Jesus Christ than they would in these wicked jungles. This assurance kept him going .

He retired to his little cabin at the stern, threw off his cloak and tricorn hat and pulled off his boots.

Picking up a sheet of paper with two verses of poetry scribbled on it, he looked out of the stern window for inspiration, first at the muddy waters of the River Sherbro and its overgrown banks, then skyward.

"Through many troubles and temptations I have already come," he murmured.

No, that didn't even fit the metre.

"Through many a danger, trouble and strife… "

No. Danger was all right. But there was the grinding hard work, too, and the temptations. Surely there was a shorter word than temptations. Trials? Lures? Snares? Hmm.

"Through many dangers, work and snares… "

That was better, but 'work' was a dull word. Travails?. Tests? Toils? Ah!

"Through many dangers, toils and snares… "

That was it! The rest of the words then flowed easily.

"Through many dangers, toils and snares, I have already come. 'Tis grace hath brought me safe thus far, and grace will lead me home."

He raised his arms to the top of the stern window,

towards the heavens.

"Praise the Lord!" he cried.

. . . .

Ross snapped awake in his bunk and his eyes shot open.

"Raise the what?"

He thought he had heard someone calling out, but soon realised he must have been dreaming, and relaxed again.

A pity, that. If he had heard the voices, he could have turned to the gorgeous Bobbie. He might do that anyway. How was she to know whether he had heard voices or not?

He looked at his watch. It was only three-thirty. He closed his eyes again but could not get back to sleep. The foul taste in his mouth did not help.

He thought of Bobbie and Lynette. How different could two women be? How his life had changed in just over a month. His thoughts of Lynette took him back six weeks, but it seemed a lifetime ago.

CHAPTER FOUR

Ross leaned back in his lounger and gazed up at the blue sky. The copious perspiration induced by Tenerife's midday sun did not bother him in the slightest. There was no big, colourful umbrella over *his* poolside table.

He was used to the heat. Twelve years in the merchant navy, mostly baking in the oven atmospheres of the Persian Gulf and the Red Sea, walking steel decks which would have blistered bare feet, had left him impervious to any discomforts the relatively moderate Canary Islands sun could inflict.

He stuck a thumb in the top of his brief bathing trunks, extended the elastic and let it snap back against the tight skin around his waist in an attempt to display self-satisfaction to any onlookers. He was only just the wrong side of thirty and had kept himself in trim.

The waiter placed a fresh gin and tonic in front of him. Ross signed the chit. He lifted the glass to eye level for a few seconds, admiring the bubbles rising from the ice and lemon, up through the blue bloom, to break on the surface. He watched the ice cube rapidly shrinking before he took a long, thirst-slaking draught.

As he put down the glass, Lynette rose out of the pool like a beautiful submarine-launched missile. Water streamed off her magnificent figure as she climbed the steps, her fine shoulders thrust back to accentuate the lift of her breasts as she gripped the handrail.

She wiggled towards Ross as if modelling the little black bikini. Two dozen pairs of male eyes lifted from magazines and cheap novels to watch. Her long, jet-black hair dripped water down onto the base of her straight back.

Ross raised his hand but the waiter was already there, ogling with all the others, as Lynette arrived at the table.

"Martini?" Ross guessed.

"No thanks, darling."   Even a refusal sounded inviting from those sensuous lips. "I'll have one of those long, fruity concoctions of yours, Carlos, with all the bits and pieces in, and lots of ice."

"Si, senora," flashed the hopeful Carlos as he lifted the tray to an exaggerated height and sped off between the tables to the bar.

Lynette pulled across a sunbed and stretched out on her back, allowing the sun to evaporate the last remaining water droplets from her tanned skin.

Ross took another gulp of his drink. Why wasn't he feeling good? It should have been the perfect set-up for a long leave. First, back in England, he had moved in with Lynette - just the two of them in that luxurious house. He had even had the use of Gordon's car. How the fool could go off to America for six months leaving a wife like Lynette behind alone was beyond Ross's understanding.

It should have been even more perfect here in the sun, halfway through their holiday. Perhaps he would have felt better if he had paid, at least for his share, instead of letting Gordon unwittingly pick up the tab.

Carlos came hurrying along. The idiot had forgotten Lynette's drink. Ross prepared to give him an earful of strong language, but there was an unusual urgency in the waiter's step as he hurried to Lynette's side.

"Senora! Senora Dewfall," he called.

Lynette raised herself on one elbow.

"Yes, Carlos. What is it?"

"Pardon, senora. Telephon."

"Telephone?" echoed Lynette. "For me?"

"Si, senora. From England. Come quickly, please."

The same two dozen pairs of eyes followed Lynette as she rose and strode off into the hotel.

Ross frowned. It couldn't be Gordon, surely? Not in England? The girls were too young to know...

He had to wait only five minutes before Lynette returned.

"I've got to go home, darling," she announced. "Emma's in hospital."

"What's the matter?"

"Appendix. She's had the operation. Nothing too serious, but I'll have to be there. Apparently, the school were trying to contact me at home all day yesterday. Muriel told them where I was. Very embarrassing. Rosanna is upset too, they want me to have her home for a week as well when Emma comes out of hospital."

"Have they sent for Gordon?"

"I don't know. You can stay on here. There's no

54

need for you to come back."

"No. Of course I can't. If Gordon's not there you'll need help. I want to be with you anyway."

The formalities at the reception desk were completed in an astonishing few minutes, the airline tickets were available to be picked up at the airport, packing took a mere quarter of an hour, by which time the taxi was waiting.

Within three hours they were airborne, heading for Heath Row.

"What if Gordon finds out?" Ross ventured as the island below reduced to atlas-view proportions.

"Finds out what?"

"That you weren't at home. That you were away on holiday with me."

"I don't care what Gordon thinks. If he can go swanning off to California for six months, leaving me with all the responsibility for the children, surely I'm entitled to a break. No, I'm more worried about what the school will say."

"But he might find out about us."

"He's bound to sooner or later."

"Why? My leave finishes in four weeks' time. I'll be away at sea long before he's due to return."

"You're not going back on those awful ships are you, darling?"

Ross had not mentioned any other possibility to Lynette, although he knew that sooner or later he would probably have to change jobs, since electronics officers were no longer wanted on many ships - cutbacks, as everywhere else. He was used to operating the ship's transmitters and receivers, using morse code, but with satellites coming in, communications could be carried out by other members of the crew in the near future. It was almost as easy as picking up the phone ashore. Technology was such that equipment was more reliable these days and it was too expensive for shipowners to employ somebody to sail with the ship simply to be there for the odd occasion when there was a breakdown. But he didn't want Lynette to know any of this - going back to sea was his perfect excuse for breaking off their relationship when the time came.

"I'll have to go back," he replied. "It's the only job I know."

Lynette gave a sigh.

"That's what Gordon said when he went off to California. Surely you could get work at home. You're an electronics man. Everybody wants them, don't they?"

"Hmm. There are a lot of people about better qualified than me, though. I don't know anything about these new computers. My certificate is only for going to sea."

"What's that? A certificate of insanity?"

Ross picked up a magazine and pretended to read. He hadn't known Lynette in a mood like this before. Edgy about her daughters, no doubt. Feeling guilty about going away, leaving them at boarding school, perhaps. He had to make allowances. Things would soon be back to normal.

Normal?

He studied her expression closely as he spoke again.

"Things aren't that bad between you and Gordon, are they? When he does come home, you and he will... well, you won't want me around then, will you?"

Lynette took his hand, squeezed it and placed it on her knee.

"Let's not talk about Gordon, darling. I don't need him now I've got you, do I?"

Ross smiled weakly and turned back to his magazine.

. . . .

Emma was discharged from hospital three days after they arrived back.

Ross was amazed at the resilience of the six-year-old to surgery. She was full of energy and took up most of Lynette's time, playing games and having stories read to her, even walks out.

There were still the nights, of course. At least then he had Lynette to himself.

Then Emma's ten-year-old sister returned. Rosanna was quieter and kept eyeing this interloper Ross with an unnerving, questioning look.

"I want to phone Daddy in America," she told Lynette on the second evening. Her eyes were fixed on Ross as she spoke, as if daring him to intervene.

"Yes, of course, darling," Lynette replied without hesitation. "I'll dial the number for you."

"I can do it, mummy."

"Can you?"

"Yes. I've got it written down."

"Oh."

The little fingers tapped out the long number.

"Don't say anything about Ross being here, or us being away, will you, darling?"

"Why not, mummy?"

"I want to tell him myself. Later. As a surprise."

Rosanna turned from her mother to Ross, giving a loud sniff as she waited for her call to be answered.

"Hello, daddy," she called excitedly, turning back to the phone. "Emma's had her 'pendix out."

Lynette seemed unconcerned about the conversation, as if she had every confidence in her daughter's obedience, but Ross, though pretending not to do so, listened to every word and intonation.

"'Bye, daddy. I love you," said Rosanna at length. "Mummy! Daddy wants to speak to you now."

Ross relaxed. Rosanna handed over the phone to Lynette and walked out past Ross, giving him a look beyond her years. He scratched the palms of his hands.

Lynette was totally calm on the telephone, conversing with her faraway husband as if she had dealt capably with a fairly mild crisis which had barely disturbed the routine of maintaining their home and awaiting his return.

Ross shuffled off upstairs to take a bath. This usually revived him, restoring his sense of wellbeing, at least temporarily, but disenchantment seemed to be lapping all around him like the bathwater.

Afterwards, he towelled himself and put on his dressing gown.

As he left the bathroom and crossed the landing to the bedroom, he heard Lynette in the girls' room. She was talking quietly, confidingly, to them. He paused outside the door to eavesdrop.

"Now, I want you to be good and get to sleep right away," Lynette was saying, "because something very exciting is going to happen soon."

"What's that, mummy?" asked Rosanna.

"It's a secret at the moment."

"Tell us the secret, mummy," begged Emma.

"Well, if you promise not to mention it to anyone else... "

"We won't, mummy, we promise," said Emma.

"All right, then," said Lynette, then paused as if to give dramatic effect to her words. "You're going to have a new daddy."

Ross placed a steadying hand on the wall.

"Won't that be exciting?" Lynette seemed puzzled by her daughters' silence.

"You don't mean this Ross?" Rosanna spoke with contemptuous disbelief.

"That's right, darling. Won't that be wonderful?"

"I want our proper daddy." Even though he could not see her, Ross visualised Emma pouting as she spoke.

"Well, he's been away a long time. Perhaps he doesn't love us any more. But Ross wouldn't go away and leave us, darling."

"Won't he go back on his ship?" asked Rosanna.

"Not when he's your daddy, darling. He'll stay with us then."

"Doesn't our real daddy want to come home?" Emma again.

"It doesn't look much like it, does it, darling?"

"Yes, he does," Rosanna declared. "He told me so on the phone. But he has to stay there at the moment because of his work."

"Is that what he told you, darling?"

"Yes. And it's true. I know."

Ross tiptoed silently off across the landing carpet to the bedroom.

. . . .

Next morning, the urge to get out of the house prompted Ross to volunteer to go out and fetch some essential groceries.

On his way back from the local supermarket a poster outside a church caught his eye.

'The wages of sin is death,' it said.

"Huh," he grunted to himself. There was more but he didn't read it.

When he arrived back, the house was empty. Lynette had left a note saying that she and the girls had been invited to a friend's house for lunch and she would be back sometime during the afternoon.

Ross dumped the shopping on the kitchen table and trudged up to the bedroom. He slumped into a hunched position on the bed and stared vacantly at the wardrobe door.

The way ahead gradually became clear. He would have to make a clean breast of the affair to Gordon, steer Lynette gently and amicably through the divorce proceedings, taking care to be scrupulously fair to Gordon as far as settlement terms were concerned. In fact, Gordon could take everything. Ross would give up the sea, make millions in the new computer boom and set up Lynette and the girls in more luxury than ever Gordon provided. He would win the girls over with his charm and generosity. He would shower them with presents and all the good things they could possibly wish for. They would want for nothing and be ever grateful to him for the wonderful way he would transform their lives.

With a shake of the head, he rose and opened the wardrobe door. It didn't take long to pack his suitcase. He took a last look round the bedroom. He would regret this, he guessed, especially after a few nights in a solitary ship's bunk, but it couldn't be allowed to go on any longer. It was better to have loved and lost than to have loved and won, that was his motto.

He left an inadequate note for Lynette before leaving and posting the key back through the letterbox.

. . . .

He stayed at an old dockside inn in Liverpool that night. The following morning found him in the tanker company's office.

"Cash in your leave, Clifford? That's not like you." The assistant marine superintendent took a genuine personal interest in the officers he had the job of assigning to the company's ships - he was one of the older school. "You've got four weeks left."

Ross had appreciated such concern in the past but would find it irksome if it continued too long this time. He looked away, his eyes flitting pointlessly around the office furniture.

"I need the money, sir. It's personal."

"I see. Well, it's lucky for both of us, then. I need an electronics officer for the Greyhound."

"The Greyhound?"

"You won't have heard of her, she's new to us. We've got her on long-term charter. She sails for the Gulf in two days. Round the Cape."

"Is she... all right?"

"What d'you mean?"

"Is she an old ship?"

"Good heavens, no. Whatever gave you that idea? You know we only charter the best."

"Right. Of course. Only last night I overheard a couple of blokes... Oh, it doesn't matter."

"Twelve months old, that's all. Monrovian registry, but she's got all the latest gear - SATCOM, SATNAV, dual rasterscan radars with ARPA. Every bit as good as our own. Two hundred thousand tonner." He lowered his voice. "Make the most of her, Clifford. You know there might not be many ships carrying electronics officers any more, don't you?"

Ross nodded. He did not want to hear all that again and changed the subject.

"And the crew?"

"Most came with the ship, but we're replacing any who leave with our own staff. What's the matter? You having second thoughts about cashing in your leave?"

"Oh, no, sir. She sounds fine."

. . . .

The *Greyhound* had been at sea for a week. They had passed the Canary Islands a couple of days earlier, where Ross had gazed without too much regret at the outline of Tenerife on the horizon. At least life was less complicated now. They were continuing southwards off the west coast of Africa, bound for the Cape and then the Gulf.

Ross was dressed only in his brief swimming trunks, with a beach towel slung over his shoulder, as he mounted the steps from the officers' deck to the bridge deck. He clutched a bottle of suntan lotion and was on his way to the monkey island for an hour's sunbathing.

It was just after lunch. He had worked hard since the ship had left Liverpool, checking all the equipment, repairing it where necessary, and now that he was satisfied everything was working well he felt he deserved some relaxation.

He paused just aft of the bridge to lean against the rail and look out to sea. The blue water rolled into white foam from the hull of the unladen tanker, spreading out into a wide wake astern which reached back as far as the eye could see.

"Every turn of the screw takes me farther from you," he muttered, absent-mindedly parodying the old saying.

"You what?"

Ross started. The third mate, who was on watch on the bridge, had come up to stand next to him.

"Oh, I didn't see you there."

"Bit early in the voyage to be talking to yourself, isn't it?"

Ross managed a weak smile.

"Have you been on this ship long, Pete?"

"Five months."

"Had any really bad passages in her?"

"In what way?"

"Any way. Bad weather? Breakdowns?"

"No. Nothing out of the ordinary. Why?"

"Oh, I overheard a couple of guys talking in a pub back in Liverpool and one was saying he'd had a terrible trip in the Greyhound."

"What did he look like?"

"I didn't actually see him. He sounded like an old guy. He definitely wasn't a captain, though. He must have been a first mate."

"There was a previous mate here, but before my time."

Ross shrugged.

"See you later, then," he said as he made for the companionway leading up to the monkey island.

The monkey island was a small deck on top of the wheelhouse, the highest deck of the ship and very popular for sunbathing. Lying on its deck, all you could see of the ship was the top of the funnel and the signal mast. The throb of the engines was barely audible. It was peaceful and no-one could look down on sunbathers there, not even the officer of the watch who was on the bridge just below.

Ross stretched himself out on the beach towel and closed his eyes.

He had not been there long when he sensed the presence of someone else. He opened one eye to see Faye, the third engineer's wife - one of the two wives on board - wrapped in her own beach towel. She smiled at Ross and he lifted a hand in greeting.

He closed his eye again. He hoped she would not start up her usual chatter, he wanted some peace. She was pleasant enough, though rather ordinary with her short brown hair and brown eyes and Geoff obviously saw something in her. But whenever Ross met her - at cabin parties, in the wardroom or whenever she sat next to him in the dining saloon - she never stopped talking, asking him all sorts of questions.

He could hear her fidgeting nearby, but it was a while before she spoke.

"Would you mind doing my back?"

Ross sighed inwardly before opening his one eye again. Then he opened the other. Faye was wearing a tiny orange bikini, revealing a trim figure he had not realised she possessed. She gave him a big smile as she held out the bottle of suntan oil towards him.

"Right."

As Ross took the bottle from her, she rolled over onto her front and unclipped the top of her bikini.

He massaged the oil into her back, daring to allow

his hand to stray round towards the sides of her breasts, then he did the backs of her legs. Familiar stirrings began to take effect, as Faye noticed with an impish grin as she turned her head towards him and lowered her eyes.

"D'you want me to do you now?"

She refastened her top as Ross laid on his front, then she massaged his back with the oil, even running her fingers inside the top of his trunks.

Ross swallowed hard. It must be a dream - he must have fallen asleep. But the pull on his arm was real enough. He turned over onto his back at her behest. She rubbed his chest and down across the tight muscles of his stomach to the top of his trunks.

She noticed his eyebrows lift.

"You must know I fancy you by now," she breathed, rubbing him.

"But Geoff... "

"Geoff's on watch in the engine-room till four o'clock," she said with a hint of urgency.

"Right. My cabin's two decks down," croaked Ross.

"I know. Come on."

Ross's pulse rate soared, as Faye took his hand and pulled as hard as she could. He rose from the deck without too much hesitation.

It always seemed to be married women. No problem, as long as it did not develop beyond pure lust. There were the advantages of a built-in excuse for keeping things temporary and the added buzz of knowing he was being compared favourably against some poor fool of a husband.

They left their towels behind and hurried down the steps and into the deck officers' accommodation.

In their haste, they failed to notice the second engineer, who was pacing the after deck below them. He frowned and began making his way towards the engine-room.

Inside Ross's cabin they had no patience for preliminaries. They pulled off each others' swimming gear and fell onto the bunk.

It was very noisy on Faye's part. Ross felt sure she would be heard on the bridge, never mind in the adjacent officers' cabins.

Afterwards, Faye seemed edgy, just wanting to get away fast - a welcome enough sign. Ross showed her to the door when they had replaced their swimming costumes. He unlocked it and began to open it.

With a bang, the door was smashed wide open by a great, hairy arm, and Geoff burst in. Faye ran out past him and began screaming hysterically.

Geoff's left arm shot out with fist clenched towards Ross's head. Ross lifted both arms to fend off the blow, failing to see Geoff's right hand.

A sledgehammer punch hit Ross low down in the groin, followed by another higher up, then a third just below the ribs.

Ross fell to the deck, gasping for breath.

Then, as Geoff stood over him, Ross saw the knife, dripping blood, in his right hand. Faye was still screaming. Geoff raised the knife until it nearly touched the deckhead, making to plunge it downwards into Ross's chest.

The third mate and the second engineer rushed in just in time to grab Geoff's arm. They wrenched the knife from his grasp and pushed him outside the cabin, where some others had gathered.

Ross looked down to see blood pouring from himself into the carpet. Then the searing pains gripped him. He cried out as the mate rushed in.

"My God!" the mate shouted. "Go and get sheets and blankets," he ordered, pulling some off the rumpled bunk and stuffing them into Ross's wounds. Ross dared not look down again.

"Send out a general call on the VHF," the mate ordered as more sheets and blankets were handed to him. "Ask for any ship with a doctor on board."

"You'll be lucky," Ross heard someone say.

"Put out an urgency signal on the SATCOM," the mate continued. "Tell the Old Man. Lock the third in the pilot's cabin and stand guard outside. More sheets!"

Ross began to feel dizzy as the pain overwhelmed him. Visions of Lynette floated before his misted eyes, also of Gordon's photograph..... Rosanna..... Emma.....

"He's going!" yelled the mate. "More blankets!"

The noises around Ross seemed to recede into the distance, the pain melted away and he felt a great peace coming over him.

The wages of sin is death, he recalled. This was it, then.

CHAPTER FIVE

Ross was aware of light. There were no images - just a general lightening of the plain curtain of his eyelids. But light from what? The light of heaven or the fires of hell? It was certainly damned hot.

He kept his eyes closed for a few moments, but he had to know sooner or later and he opened them slowly.

An electric light with a plain shade was hanging from a high ceiling. A large-bladed electric fan rotated slowly next to the lamp. Neither looked particularly heavenly nor threatening.

Suddenly a black face blocked out anything else he might have seen. It was a woman's face. She was about forty, Ross guessed, but had a pretty smile, dimpled cheeks and sparkling, popping eyes.

"Welcome back to the land of the living, Mister Clifford," she beamed with a rich, happy loudness. "You're lucky. Do you know where you are?"

The nurse's cap was unmistakable.

"Hos... "

"That's right. Hospital."

"Where?"

"Freetown, Mister Clifford. Sierra Leone."

"Oh."

He closed his eyes again. That was enough for now.

Next time Ross awoke the same nurse was on hand again. She chatted incessantly. Her name was Yema and she had been assigned to him because of her good English. "London trained," she claimed proudly.

"You were very lucky," she kept telling him. "You had good first aid treatment and they got you here just in time. The hospital only last week received a new shipment of supplies - aid from Britain - so there was anaesthetic for you. The very first use of it was on a Britisher - you!" She let out a great guffaw.

Ross smiled a thin smile which he hoped conveyed his thanks. Now he remembered the circumstances.

"Am I going to be all right, nurse?" he asked.

"Of course," Yema assured him. "You had the best surgeon in Freetown, you lucky man."

"I mean, will I be all right... you know... down there?"

Yema shrieked with laughter.

"No doubt about it, you will be able to live life to the full in a month or two, you naughty man!"

Ross closed his eyes in relief, then lapsed into a doze again.

Within two days he was able to sit up in bed, survey the dingy ward and take some watery milk rather than the drip.

Yema chatted to him almost non-stop, about her husband and three girls and how well they were doing, even in such hard times. She seemed to put in a lot of hours - she was there early in the morning and still there late at night and Ross wondered how she could remain so cheerful in such dreary surroundings, and if she ever went home.

The shipping agent, Mr. Bonema-Jarvis, a portly, middle-aged African in a smart black tropical suit, paid him a visit. He filled Ross in with the details of what had happened. The mate had done a good job of first aid and the ship had made Freetown in time. The agent's speech was very rapid and he tended to mumble and Ross had to stop and think what he had said each time before speaking himself.

"What happened to the third engineer?"

"Flown home in handcuffs with a police escort to face charges. Attempted murder, you understand. His wife went too, of course, but they weren't speaking. A replacement third is being flown out to Cape Town. The ship will have to put in there."

"And a replacement electronics officer?" queried Ross.

"No. The company didn't think it necessary. They can operate the SATCOM themselves. They're going to do away with electronics officers soon anyway. If the equipment breaks down it will have to be fixed at the next port. Cost-cutting, you understand."

Ross nodded. He had heard all the same arguments hundreds of times. It was inevitable - but not yet, surely?

"What will happen to me?" he asked.

"A few weeks' rest and recuperation first, then when you're fit enough we'll either fly you home or put you on board a ship going in that direction. You'll be travelling D.B.S., you understand. You'll be needed to testify at the trial."

"Right.   Make it a ship," Ross pleaded.   The thought of having to face a trial, let alone Geoff and Faye, filled him with dismay.   He might have Lynette and Gordon to confront, too.   And Rosanna.   The longer he could put it off the better.

"I'll do my best," promised the agent.   "But first you must recover your health and strength."

The improvement in Ross's condition was depressingly rapid.   Within a week he was wheeling himself around the wards in a wheelchair and sitting out on the verandah where he could see the world going by along the busy road.

After a few days of this, however, Ross began to feel more restless.   The pains had almost gone, leaving only a certain stiffness, and he was eating well, although the diet of rice with very little else made him long even for the efforts of the *Greyhound*'s cook.   He could also walk unaided.

Yema noticed his fidgeting, as she noticed everything else about him.

"I think it's time you had a little trip away from this place, Mister Clifford," she said to him one day.   "It's my youngest daughter's fifteenth birthday tomorrow and we're having a party with all the family there.   Would you like to join us?"

A party!   That was more like it.

"Right.   Thank you very much," he enthused.   "That would be great."

. . . .

Ross was collected in an old Datsun which billowed blue smoke and showed further outward signs of prolonged neglect. Yema introduced the driver as her husband, Hubert. He looked much older than Yema and not nearly so jolly.

They passed through residential areas comprising two-storey apartment blocks and whitewashed bungalows reminiscent of holiday camp chalets, but the house they pulled up at was a rather grand affair, although it had seen better days. It was an old two-storey red-painted stone house with a wide external staircase, its banister supported by thick stone pillars, which led to a large upper balcony of similar design.

Ross was led into a big room on the ground floor, almost devoid of furniture, although he was given a chair himself. It was crowded with Yema's extended family, all obviously dressed up in their best clothes, especially the women in their bright, colourful dresses and headscarves.

Ross was treated as a visiting celebrity. He was plied with palm wine and food - the inevitable rice but this time with spicy meats and vegetables mixed in, which made it much more palatable than the hospital fare.

There was distorted music from a small cassette player and tribal-style dancing. The highlight of the evening was a solo dance by Yehu, the birthday girl herself.

There was no mistaking Yema's daughter, with the same dimpled cheeks and sparkling, popping eyes. Barefoot, she wore a skimpy, slit brown skirt, which revealed flashes of shapely legs, and a gold-coloured top of wide-mesh net which made no serious attempt to hide the firm, upward-tilting breasts beneath. A white sash around her waist and white headgear completed her dress. The dance was provocative, with much high-kicking and hip-thrusting, encouraged by clapping from the onlookers.

It may have been Ross's imagination, but he felt the girl was deliberately directing the dance at himself, flirting with him. Wishful thinking, perhaps, but her sparkling eyes seemed to be on him all the time, as if challenging him to deny he was being aroused. If so, it was working. Yema was right, everything was functioning well in the engine-room.

One day, when Ross was a successful theatrical agent, he would return for Yehu and arrange worldwide bookings for her exotic dancing: London, Paris, New York, Las Vegas... She would take the world by storm and they would both make millions.

After Yehu's dance, the effects of the palm wine suddenly rendered Ross incapable of further cohesive thought or action. He could vaguely recall Yehu sitting on his knee and calling him Uncle Ross and Yema fussing over him, worried that she had failed in her professional responsibility by not keeping a closer watch over his intake of alcohol. He remembered being bundled back into the car - then nothing else.

· ·

Ross awoke in his hospital bed - his head hurting more than the diminishing discomfort from his operation.

Yema was soon there.

"How are you feeling, Mister Clifford?"

"Terrible."

"Oh dear. Don't let anyone know, or I'll be in big trouble. I should have realised you wouldn't be used to our wine."

"Don't worry, I won't let you down. I had a really great time last night. Thanks for inviting me - I hope I didn't disgrace myself too much."

"Oh, no, Mister Clifford. All my family were so happy to see you there. And Yehu took a real liking to you. She's thrilled at having a new Uncle Ross from England."

"I thought your daughter was delightful," said Ross, hoping that he had not revealed the darker thoughts he harboured of the nubile young dancer.

Mr. Bonema-Jarvis called in the afternoon, by which time Ross was in better spirits.

"I'll be putting you on board a ship in about ten days' time," announced the agent. "She'll be sailing for Felixstowe after about three days here, you understand. You'll have a further week's recuperation time on the voyage home."

Ross smiled thinly, then closed his eyes for a second. Oh, God! he cried inwardly, please don't let me be sent back yet.

"That's very thoughtful of you," he said. "Thanks."

Then, a few days later, Yema failed to appear. Another nurse who could speak no understandable

English brought him his food. He wandered around the hospital and out onto the verandah, but there was no sign of her.

"She's indisposed," a doctor told him rather unhelpfully when he finally found someone who could speak good enough English.

Two days later Yema reappeared, but in ordinary clothes rather than her nurse's uniform. There was no big smile - instead tears filled her eyes as she came up to Ross sitting in his wicker chair on the verandah. He suddenly felt sick - her seniors must have found out about the party and she had had the sack.

Tears still flowed as she spoke.

"Yehu's gone missing, Mister Clifford," she cried out loudly.

Ross stood and placed his hands on her heaving shoulders as she sobbed. He looked hard into her distraught face.

"How do you mean, missing?" He spoke quietly, calmly.

"She didn't come home from school," Yema wailed. "That was two days ago. The whole family's been out searching for her, and the police."

"Haven't you any idea where she might be?"

It was a silly thing to say, but he had never been called upon to offer comfort to anyone in anything like such circumstances before.

"Oh, I can't bear to think of it, Mister Clifford. Some kids go off - with a man or to get drugs or... " The sobbing increased in intensity. "... Or into prostitution.

76

Some are never heard of again."

Yema's next howl caused other patients and staff to look across. Their faces were blank and helpless, concerned but impotent. Yema's drawn features were in such sharp contrast to her previous beaming smiles.

"I'll help you look for her," said Ross confidently. "I'll be able to look in places you can't."

Yema squeezed his hand in desperate gratitude.

Ross was now free to come and go as he pleased. He wandered the streets, particularly in the more seedy areas, looking for a young, nimble girl with dimpled cheeks and popping, sparkling eyes.

He approached every dockside pimp and was taken to a range of apartments - some disgusting hovels and others relatively sumptuous brothels - but none of the girls he was shown bore any resemblance to the vivacious Yehu, even though he always asked for their newest and youngest. He suffered angry verbal abuse from pimps, madams and the women themselves as they realised he was not a bona fide customer, but he was unrepentant and continued relentlessly for three days and nights.

At last, having scoured what must have been the entire vice community of Freetown, he had to admit defeat and flopped into his hospital bed once more.

He moped around the hospital for two more days, trying unsuccessfully to comfort Yema on the few occasions she made an appearance. He racked his brains to try to think of something more he could do or say which might help, but she had already thought of everything he suggested.

Then, as he was sitting out on his wicker chair on the verandah, wearing his dressing-gown, she announced the arrival of a visitor, and Captain Bridson entered Ross's life.

. . . .

Ross must have dropped off to sleep. His first reaction was to look at his watch. Nearly five o'clock.

With a gasp, he leapt out of his bunk, pulled on his shorts and shirt and shot off barefoot for the radio office. He would just catch the schedule with WCH.

It was a close-run thing and there was a message for them. Lucky he had not missed it or Captain Bridson would have had another tantrum. It was all in code again.

Ross returned to his cabin to finish dressing, then set out to find the captain. This time Bridson was in his cabin. He took the message without comment.

Later, as Ross was freshening up before dinner, Captain Bridson poked his head round Ross's cabin door.

"We sail at two tomorrow," he announced.

"For the Plantains?" queried Ross.

"The what?"

"I thought I heard somebody say we were sailing for somewhere that sounded like the Plantains."

"No," the captain growled irritably. "Charleston, South Carolina. I told you before."

"Oh, yes. Right."

Bobbie was at dinner, but Ross was not sitting near enough to her to engage her in conversation. She was talking with Bridson but Ross could not overhear.

Back in his cabin, he gazed out of his window across the deck, hoping to see her take an evening stroll again.

It seemed an age, and Ross was about to give up, when his patience was rewarded.

She walked elegantly to the ship's side rail and gazed out over the water, looking like Grace Kelly at the peak of her screen career.

Ross ran down the stairs and out onto the deck. She would not get away this time.

"Don't jump! He's not worth it," Ross quipped as he approached her.

"Oh. Hi." The warm smile was encouraging.

"D'you usually come out on deck after dinner?"

"Ah like to take the evening air. You too?"

"Right." Ross stood as close to her as he could without actual contact, close enough to be aware of her perfume. "Mind you, I prefer to survey the world from that little verandah outside the wardroom, enjoying a gin and tonic."

"Ian will keep you company there, although he's a whisky person."

"What about you?"

"Oh, ah don't drink much. An occasional Bacardi and coke, mebbe."

"Well, let's make this one of those occasions, then. Come up and join me in a drink and tell me all about yourself."

For the first time, Bobbie showed the slightest sign of being flustered.

"Oh, ah'm sorry, Ross. Now that we're sailing tomorrow, ah have some paperwork to get finished. Some other time, mebbe."

It was a feeble excuse. There couldn't be any work for a doctor to do here. No-one was even sick, as far as Ross knew.

"Okay, but I'll hold you to that."

"Sure," she smiled. "Now, if you'll excuse me.." She backed away, as if afraid of Ross.

"Right. See you, Bobbie. Mind how you go."

She turned and walked off back towards the accommodation. The gentle swaying of her hips triggered an unuttered groan deep within Ross.

That went well then! Ross's wry thought chastised him for too abrupt an approach.

After she had disappeared, he went to the wardroom to have a drink before retiring to his bunk. He would have to test all the equipment again before sailing, so he would take an early night.

. . . .

John Newton stood out in the middle of the deck, feet well apart, his tricorn hat at a jaunty angle and his cloak curling round the tops of his boots, staring downstream. He licked a finger and held it up to test the wind direction.

His friend the surgeon approached.

"Ye seem anxious to get under way from here, captain."

"Aye, Robert. Our business here is finished. The

80

next favourable wind during daylight and by the grace of God we shall haul down for the Plantains. A land breeze oft springs up at the ebb after the sun passes its zenith. I sense the morrow will provide the conditions we seek."

"Ye know these parts well, sir."

"Aye, I should do, Robert. Not least the Plantains. Near twelve months I tarried there against my own will and, I believe, God's. A slave – no more, no less, was I – and to this very Mister Clow with whom I am about to do business."

Robert Arthur had heard the story many times before, but he knew better than to stop the captain re-living his terrible experiences aloud to anyone who would listen.

"It began civilized enough with myself in Clow's employ," Newton resumed. "But evil men and Clow's African wife, who disliked me from the start, I know not why, convinced Clow of my supposed dishonesty and worthlessness. I became grievously ill of the fever and, rather than the kindness I would have expected, received naught but cruelty – starvation, neglect and sarcastic words. I was left for long periods under the control of the wife, Pee Eye by name, while Clow traveled on business, and at these times my predicament was even worse. Two things alone kept me sane, Robert: a study of a book on Euclid mathematics, which I contrived to secrete from my tormentors, and the task of planting thousands upon thousands of lime trees, which still flourish to this day on the islands. Finally, by the grace of God, I was rescued by some friends of my father."

"I wonder ye can do business now with the like of such folk, sir."

"God has forgiven me much more, Robert, so I must forgive them – 'tis the Lord's command."

"Ye be a saint for so doing, sir."

"Nay, Robert, merely the same slave doing the bidding of his new master, and rejoicing in the wonder of it all."

"Thee be blessed, sir."

"Aye, Robert. But you are weary now. I see you stifle a yawn."

"Nay, sir."

"Get off to your bed, Robert, for we sail tomorrow, God willing."

"Aye-aye, sir."

As Robert Arthur left his captain alone on the deck, Newton turned and ambled aft, humming a tune as he went, which soon turned into an open song.

"Unless the Lord had been my stay
With trembling joy my soul may say
My cruel foe had gain'd his end:
But he appeared for my relief,
And Satan sees, with shame and grief,
That I have an almighty Friend."

Ross stirred in his bunk and cocked an ear. He had heard correctly. It was singing - out on deck.

"Oh, 'twas a dark and trying hour,
When, harassed by the tempter's power,
I felt my strongest hopes decline… "

Ross ran to the window but stopped himself from

opening it.

"You only who have known his arts,
You only who have felt his darts,
Can pity such a case as mine."

Ross slipped on his dressing gown, ran out of his cabin and along the alleyway where he pounded on the surgeon's door. There was no sound of a response, so he opened the door and looked in. The cabin was empty. The computer screen displayed a moving green pattern.

"Damn!" he cried and ran back to his cabin, but the singing had stopped anyway.

He lowered the shutter and peered out. There was no-one on deck. All was quiet.

He threw off his dressing gown and climbed wearily back into his bunk.

CHAPTER SIX

The following morning saw the deck hands preparing the ship for sea, battening down the hatches and generally tidying the decks.

Ross re-tested all the electronic equipment, the captain and mate pored over the Atlantic charts and there were humming and clanking noises from the engine-room.

They were due to sail at two o'clock.

. . . .

Right on time, the rattling winch hauled up the *Duke*'s anchor and the engines began to throb.

Slowly, the ship moved down river, its screw churning up mud which was then left behind in the rippling wake. Not much clearance beneath the keel, Ross suspected, even though they had waited for high tide.

Ross went into the radio office and tapped a message out in morse code to inform Freetown of their departure: DUKE OF ARGYLL LEAVING RIVER SHERBRO BOUND CHARLESTON, SOUTH CAROLINA.

He had barely received the brief acknowledgment when he was startled by a great bellow from behind.

"What the flaming hell do you think you're doing, Mister Clifford?"

Ross turned to see Captain Bridson standing in the

doorway, his face quivering with rage.

"Just sending our TR, sir."

"Our *what*?"

"Traffic report, sir. Just letting Freetown know we're sailing and where to."

The captain stepped up to Ross and put his lip-curling face right up to Ross's.

"Blast you! Don't you ever do anything like that again, d'you hear?"

"It's normal practice, sir."

"Not on my ship, it isn't! No transmitter, and that includes the SATCOM, is to be used without my express permission. **Is that clear**?"

"Yes, sir."

"You will see to it that my orders are obeyed in this respect as in all others, **will you not**?"

"Yes, sir."

The captain stamped off back to the bridge.

Ross had heard stories of eccentric passenger ship captains, but had never expected to have to sail with one.

He tuned in to WCH at the appointed time but there was no message.

He wandered out on deck to watch the scenery. They passed close to Bonthe, a town on Sherbro Island at the river's mouth, where an odd mixture of new and ramshackle old buildings stood side by side along the waterfront. Then the river mouth widened into open sea, although the ship stayed close to the mainland shore, steering northward to avoid some dangerous shoals.

The captain came thumping along the deck and

Ross braced himself for another verbal assault, but Bridson simply handed him a long coded message to send to WCH. Apart from the radio station call letters, there was no address, which was most unusual. When Ross queried it, he was told gruffly that his job was to send whatever the captain gave him without question. Ross made a mental note to remind the captain of his words if ever there was an error in a transmitted message.

This one was not much easier to decipher than the one Ross had received before. The date and time of their departure from the River Sherbro was plain enough, but the rest was figures and letter groups with no obvious meaning.

Dinner was early, to fit in with a relatively quiet stretch in their passage between unfamiliar shoals, rocks and islands. Officers came and went hurriedly as they relieved each other on their watches. Bobbie was there but she avoided his gaze. He made several attempts at small talk with her but these were inhibited by the presence of Ian and two engineers and she was unresponsive. The captain and mate were on the bridge.

Suddenly, the engine vibrations became louder. The second engineer cocked an ear to listen. Crockery began to rattle.

The engineers quickly vacated the table as they rushed off below, leaving their plates and cutlery doing a dance to the throbbing rhythm.

The alarm bells rang. Ian jumped up from the table.

"Yon stupid sods must have put her aground," he

grumbled as he dashed out, leaving Bobbie and Ross.

"I'll have to go and stand by in the radio office," Ross said, jumping up and running out.

Ross hovered between the radio office, the chartroom and the bridge, all within a few paces of each other, to try to overhear what was going on. He discovered that they had not run aground but would have to anchor due to engine trouble.

The engine stopped and all became quiet again. They were drifting off the shore of a small island, with a lovely long, low beach and palm trees behind. It was just like the popular concept of the desert island.

A deafening clatter turned Ross's eyes to the bows to see a cloud of rust rising from the winch as the released chain permitted the anchor to fall. At least they should not drift onto the shore now.

The chief engineer, wearing a boiler suit, came up to the bridge to report to the captain.

"Main bearing trouble, skipper."

Captain Bridson winced at the title the chief bestowed upon him.

"Can you fix it?"

"We can replace the thrust pads, but there's a problem with the oil feed that we'll have to sort out too."

"How long?"

"At least twentyfour hours."

"Blast!" said the captain. "Could you not have seen to it while we were in port?"

"These things happen without warning, skip. Everything was all right until half an hour ago."

"Oh, very well. Get it done. Pull out all the flaming stops."

"Okay, skip."

The chief left the bridge. Captain Bridson turned to the mate, who was drawing lines on the chart.

"Where are we?"

"A quarter mile off shore, old fruit."

"What's that island?"

"One of the Plantains."

Ross's eyebrows lifted. He recalled the voices from the previous night. 'We sail for the Plantains on the afternoon tide.' Isn't that what the voice supposedly belonging to the man Newton had said? Could somebody have known this was going to happen?

Ross did not feel able to tell anyone what he had heard, not even Bobbie. He doubted whether they would believe him and he had no proof.

As the captain and mate walked out onto the bridge, Ross peered at the chart. The Plantains were just off a promontory of the mainland coast.

The captain returned with a message for Ross.

"Get this off to WCH at the first opportunity," he growled.

"Yes, sir."

"Not a good start, eh?"

"No, sir."

"We've barely covered fifty flaming miles."

"Better to happen here than in mid-Atlantic, sir."

"True."

This time the message was in plain language but

still without an address: ENGINE FAILURE 1835 HOURS 26 JUNE STOP EXPECT DELAY 24 HOURS MINIMUM STOP SHIP SAFE AT ANCHOR STOP CARGO SECURE.

After sending the message, Ross went below to the wardroom, poured himself a gin and tonic and signed the chit.

Darkness had fallen rapidly and Ross gazed out in the direction of the Plantain Islands. Two lights twinkled, so they were not entirely uninhabited. He breathed in the evening air.   Delicate scents were borne along by the gentle breeze - familiar, yet Ross was not able to identify them straight away. He sniffed the air deeply.   Citrus fruit. Lemons? Limes? He shivered, despite the heat.

He looked across the decks hoping for a glimpse of Bobbie, but the only person he saw was a deckhand walking aft.

He could go and invite her for a drink in the wardroom. Why not?

There was no response to his knock on her door. He grasped the handle but did not turn it. He checked the dining saloon - empty - then returned to his own cabin.

Lying fully clothed on his bunk, he closed his eyes and waited expectantly, listening. He was silently willing the voices to start again, but there was no sound.

He must have dozed off. When he awoke he could hear the familiar voice outside. He sat up.

"The Plantain Islands, Mister Bridson.   Do ye smell those limes on the night air? I planted those lime trees myself, Mister Bridson, while I was kept in conditions of the utmost depravity. My two tormentors - the very pair I have oft mentioned to you - are coming aboard this evening - what do you think of that?"

"If I had been treated by them as you were, cap'n, I should throw them overboard, or better still add them to the cargo below."

"Nay, Mister Bridson, I shall show them the greatest complaisance and kindness and if they have any shame they will feel sorry for their former ill treatment of me. They will receive no condemnation from me. Vengeance is mine, saith the Lord. So prepare to receive them - Mister Clow and his African wife."

"Aye-aye, sir."

"They will see our meeting as a strange quirk of fate, but I see the work of the Almighty here, Mister Bridson, designed to bring them to repentance of their sins, I believe... "

Ross had been so preoccupied with the conversation that he had briefly forgotten why he had been wishing for it.

Now he jumped up from the bunk, ran out of his cabin and along the alleyway, where he hammered on the surgeon's door. This time he opened it after a split second of silence, but again she was not there. He rushed up and down stairs, looking and listening for her, but she was nowhere to be seen or heard. Where the devil did she get to?

He went back to his cabin and listened again.

"Welcome aboard, Mister Clow."

"Greetings, John-lad."

"And your good lady. Welcome, madam."

"My oath! John-lad, what a transformation in thee fortunes. What a fine vessel. And thee as master."

"The Lord has been kind to me, Mister Clow."

"Dost recall my prophecy of this?"

"I do indeed."

"Many a true word spoken in jest, eh?"

"I had not realised you had been jesting, Mister Clow."

The two men laughed.

"So now let us talk of trade."

"See, John-lad, I have some fine merchandise for 'ee."

"Come below, then. I may just find some of your favourite brandy in my room."

The conversation ended, Ross dashed to the window and released the shutter. It took a moment for his eyes to adjust to the dimly-lit deck outside, but this time he just caught sight of the back of a figure disappearing into the crew accommodation aft. All he had seen was a man's lower leg, wearing a boot, and a dark coat reaching down to calf-length, which looked vaguely familiar.

So there was somebody! One of the crew from aft, most likely.

Ross flopped back on the bunk, a smile of relief escaping from his lips.

It was in a happier state of mind that, shortly afterwards, he set his alarm, got undressed and climbed into his bunk.

He was awakened from a deep sleep by raised

voices out on deck.

"Au revoir, then, John-lad. I trust thee will reach Antigua safely and have a prosperous voyage."

Antigua? Had Ross heard correctly? Even allowing for a sleep-dazed brain, he could hardly have misheard Antigua for Charleston.

"Thank you, Mister Clow, I shall hope for more business with you next time I visit the coast, a year or two hence, God willing."

"Aye, by all means. Bygones be bygones, eh?"

Ross looked at his alarm clock. It was two-fifteen in the morning.

He resisted the temptation to lower his window shutter and hurriedly got dressed. He'd catch the bastards on deck this time.

His feet barely brushed the stairs as he vaulted himself down by the handrails.

Out on deck there was no-one to be seen, nor was there any sound.

Ross strode down the deck to the crew quarters and looked around, but all the cabins were in darkness.

Up and down the deck he paced angrily before returning to his cabin.

As he began to undress again, a man's voice began singing. This time the song was familiar.

> *"Amazing grace, how sweet the sound*
> *That saved a wretch like me.*
> *I once was lost but now am found,*
> *Was blind but now I see."*

Ross quickly pulled his clothes back on as the

song continued.

"'Twas grace that taught my heart to fear..."

Ross raced down the alleyway and banged on the surgeon's door. There was no response. Taking a deep breath, he flung the door open and switched on the light.

The cabin was empty. The computer screen still flickered the idling display.

Ross switched off the light and backed out. If she was not in her own cabin at this time of night, it could mean only one thing. But whose? He shuffled, shoulders hunched, back to his cabin, where the song was still continuing.

"Yes, when this flesh and heart shall fail
And mortal life shall cease... "
I shall possess, within the veil,
A life of joy and peace."

Wearily, Ross lowered the shutter and peered out. There was nothing to be seen, but the singing continued. The voice seemed to rise from directly below his window. Or was it from above? He stuck his head out and looked all around. Whoever it was must be hiding behind one of the hold ventilators.

He pulled up the shutter. No-one was going to give him any more run-around tonight. He undressed and got back into his bunk.

"The earth shall soon dissolve like snow,
The sun forbear to shine;
But God who called me here below
Will be forever mine."

Ross pulled the bedclothes over his head and shut

his eyes tightly.

CHAPTER SEVEN

In the morning, Ross strolled around the decks, trying to see any likely hiding places for anyone who might be attempting to torment him. There were two ventilator outlets, one either side of the ship's centre line. They were big enough to hide behind - about five feet high with sides three feet long - steel boxes with a grille near the top of each, through which Ross could hear the hum of electric fans. They would provide air for number two hold.

Another likely place was directly beneath his window. He had not noticed it before, but the cabins on the officers' decks overhung those on the main deck below, leaving a kind of shelter on the main deck. Someone in there, pressed against the bulkhead, would not be seen from the cabin windows above.

Then there was the crew accommodation aft, but normal voices would not carry that far and still be clear enough for him to hear every word.

That left three hiding places only: the two ventilators and the shelter beneath his cabin window.

He gazed across the water to the Plantain Island. It would have made a good picture for the front of a travel brochure. Could anybody really have come aboard from there last night?

What he wanted next was a good excuse to go and have a snoop around the crew quarters aft, where he had seen the back of a figure disappearing.

He wandered into the radio office and listened for WCH, but there was nothing. He studied his copy of the crew list, but that is all it was - just a list of names.

Then his eyes alighted on a grey box in the corner of the radio office - a box with a single red lamp glowing in the centre of its front panel. The communal aerial! That was it! His excuse.

The communal aerial was a booster amplifier fed from one of the ship's aerials. Its output was along cables to a connection box in every cabin on the ship. The cabin's occupant could plug his radio into it as an aerial, since radios would not receive anything within the steel confines of the accommodation. As the radio officer, he could enter anybody's cabin to inspect their aerial connection box for maintenance or repairs.

So that afternoon he set about inspecting the crew's aerial connection boxes. He had the crew list with him and plenty of time to look around each cabin while he pretended to clean inside each box.

Some of the crew were not in their cabins, but the pictures and articles around the rooms revealed quite a lot about them.

Seaman Jamie Gallagher was obviously a musical man, with a guitar in the corner and pictures of pop groups around the bulkheads. There was nothing which would suggest an interest in hymns though.

Not a thing was out of place in bo's'n John Hallin's room. All the pictures were of ships and there were a few ornaments in the shape of nautical museum pieces.

By contrast, the cook - or chef, as Captain Bridson liked to call him - had a cabin which might have belonged to an unruly teenager. Mark Couture was half French.

Ross met a number of people who were in their cabins when he called. Most were from Liverpool.

Joe Fellows, the officers' steward, he had seen many times before, serving in the dining saloon and cleaning around the officers' cabins. He was about thirty.

Seaman Bill Barber was in his forties. He spoke with a more cultured accent than most. There was a picture of himself in officer's uniform, so he had obviously come down in the world for some reason.

"Giddy" Meacham was a much older man of the seadog breed. Ross felt he must be well past normal retiring age, unless his white whiskers made him look much older than he was. He had some nice pictures on his walls - mostly country scenes, but there was one of Salisbury Cathedral.

The other seamen were in their early twenties, fugitives from the dole office. The two engine-room ratings were working below. Their cabins told Ross little but he had seen them around, very noticeable in their dirty boiler-suits, and they were also both twenty-something.

By dusk the engine was running again, the anchor was hauled up and the ship was under way on its anticipated two-week voyage to Charleston. The Plantain Islands rapidly receded into the gloom. The echo sounder, drawing its graph of the sea bottom, indicated shallow water for a while, then the image rapidly plunged until it was beyond the range of the instrument. The trace of the coastline of Africa on the radar display became less and less distinct until suddenly there was nothing left to see and the mate switched it off, turning to stare out of the bridge windows into the empty blackness. The little ship was alone in the vastness of the Atlantic Ocean.

Ross received weather reports – severe storms in mid-Atlantic but a long way ahead - and sent another message to WCH, no doubt informing them of the *Duke*'s departure, but again all in code groups.

It was good to be at sea again, with the cool air provided by the ship's forward movement circulating through the accommodation. A ship in port always had a stale smell about it. The throb of engines and the swish of slate blue water rolling away from the ship's sides gave everyone on board a new sense of purpose.

The sea was calm, the gentle swell giving a slight motion which did little more than provide a certain springiness to Ross's feet as he took a stroll round the deck after dinner. Bobbie did not appear.

During the next three days the whole ship seemed to settle into an almost sleepy routine. Work for everyone was minimal. The watchkeepers on the bridge had nothing to look at. The engines rumbled on reliably, driving the ship along at a steady fifteen knots. The crew were kept gently occupied on deck, chipping and painting patches of rusting railings and bulkheads.

Ross listened out for WCH but there was never a message. He took weather reports of the storms in the Atlantic but the *Duke* was steering a more southerly course than she would have otherwise followed in order to avoid them. Ian explained that the *Duke* was small and not built for the worst weather the north Atlantic could throw at her. Ross was grateful for the decision, although a little surprised as it would make the voyage a day longer – or even two. He spent most of his leisure time sunbathing by day and reading at night.

Bobbie proved to be extremely elusive. Despite the clement weather, he could not catch her out on deck. He only seemed to see her at meal times where it was impossible to chat her up. He tried knocking on her cabin door many times but there was never any response, yet he was sure she was in there on some of these occasions. When he did try the door several times, it was always locked. Surely his clumsy approach when they were on the coast could not have been so offensive as to put her off him altogether, could it? Perhaps Ian was wrong and there was somebody else in her life after all.

In the wardroom, Ross briefly scanned the books on the shelves of the glass cabinet that made claim to be the ship's library. They were all very old - probably never changed since the ship was new. He picked out a detective novel without much deliberation - it was only a means off lulling him off to sleep. He could examine the other titles more carefully some other time.

Naked in his bunk, he found the book less than gripping and he was soon dozing off. He laid the book aside and prepared to go to sleep.

"In the midst of life we are in death," came the voice from outside the window, this time loud and solemn. "Of whom may we seek for succour, but of thee,

O Lord, who for our sins art justly displeased."

Ross leapt out of bed and pulled on his shorts as the voice continued to intone in melancholy phrases.

He would not open the window, but run downstairs and try to surprise whoever it was on deck, hoping for better success this time.

Just as he was about to leave the cabin, however, he froze. The words that were being spoken had a familiar ring about them and the hairs on his neck seemed to rise in response to an electric charge as he listened.

"Forasmuch as it hath pleased Almighty God of his great mercy to take unto himself the soul of our dear brother, John Bridson, here departed: we therefore commit his body to the deep... "

Ross heard a scraping sound, then a pause, then a splash, before the voice continued.

"... earth to earth, ashes to ashes, dust to dust; in sure and certain hope of the Resurrection to eternal life, through our Lord Jesus Christ; who shall change our vile body, that it may be like unto his glorious body... "

Ross collected himself together and dashed off through the door, tumbled down the stairs and out onto the darkened deck.

He fumbled his way to the nearest ventilator housing, then the other one, then back to the shelter beneath his window. There was no voice now and Ross found no-one there, although it was almost pitch-dark and whoever might have been there could easily have slipped away unnoticed.

Ross went along to the crew quarters. Lights were

on in most of the cabins but he had no excuse for intruding this time.

He made his way back to his own cabin, kicked off his shorts and got back into bed.

Bridson dead? No, it was impossible. Ross would have been told. News like that could not have been kept secret for more than an hour. There would have been a message to send. Ross had seen him around the ship that day. Someone out there was definitely trying to wind him up again. He turned to try and get some sleep.

Almost as soon as his head touched the pillow, the voices began again. Ross sat up, angry.

"All quiet, Mister Marshall?"

"Aye, sir. All be well and quiet."

"Good."

"It be dreadful calm, though, sir."

"It is indeed."

"At this rate, our middle passage will take five weeks or more."

"'Tis as the Lord wills, Samuel."

Ross jumped up again, this time grabbing a towel to wrap around himself as he ran out and along the alleyway.

"Ross! What is it?" The surgeon was at home this time and had answered Ross's urgent knock almost instantly.

"The voices," he gasped. "Come on."

She hurried after him, the clip-clip of her shoes on the deck contrasting with the thud-thud of his bare feet.

He threw the cabin door wide open, took her hand

and led her to the shuttered window. He held up the forefinger of his free hand to his lips and they both listened intently.

"I knew this would happen," he said after a few seconds. "It's Sod's Law, isn't it?"

"Shh."

"Can you hear something, then?"

"No. But let's give them a chance."

They stood together for what seemed an incredibly long time, but was probably only a minute or two. He still held her hand and felt the tenseness in her breathing. He watched her bosom heaving beneath the plain white dress. He could not help but notice her wide blue eyes, her long silky blonde hair and her full red lips, parted slightly in anticipation of any slight sound from outside.

"You're right, Ross," she said at length. "If there were voices, they've stopped."

"If? D'you think I'm imagining them, then?"

She ignored the question.

"What were the voices saying this time?"

"Oh, just about the weather. They were saying the voyage might take five weeks."

"My, it would have to be really bad if we're going to take that long."

"But the weather was calm, they said. Just as it is."

"Any storms forecast ahead?"

"Well, yes, but several days' steaming away, and we're going more to the south to avoid them. There's nothing that would delay us for weeks. I must be going doolally," he concluded glumly. He backed off telling her of the funereal speech he had heard previously. That would be too much for her to swallow. She would have known of anything wrong with Bridson.

He felt her pulling at his fingers. He looked down. He had not realised he was still holding on to her hand, and so tightly too."

"Oh, sorry."

"That's all right, Ross," she said as she freed herself.

"I think I need a stiff drink," he said. "Would you like to join me in the wardroom?"

"I have a better idea, Ross." She went to the door, pushed it to and clicked the lock into place, then turned back to face him.

Slowly, she began unbuttoning her dress from the top, revealing a lacy white bra beneath. As she continued unbuttoning downwards, she spoke.

"If there are voices in your head, Ross, I think I know how to drive them away."

The dress parted at the front like a pair of curtains, revealing her creamy-white legs and white panties. With a slight shrug, the dress fell off her shoulders and on to the floor at her feet.

She kicked off her white high-heeled shoes.

Putting her hands behind her back, she unclipped the bra and that too fell to the floor. Ross gulped.

"Bobbie!" he breathed.

Slowly, she placed the tips of her thumbs into the waistband of her panties and wriggled them down her lovely legs.

Briefly, she stood upright before him in her naked splendour, then stepped across to him.

With the speed of a whiplash, she tugged the towel from around him and threw it across to the far side of the cabin.

Pushing him onto the bunk, she looked down and moistened her lips with her tongue.

He moved over to allow her to join him on the narrow bunk. He put his arms around her and drew her against himself, bringing his face up to hers.

She placed a hand across his mouth.

"No kissing, Ross."

"What?"

"I don't want to be kissed, Ross."

Their bodies wrapped themselves around each other. It did not seem natural to Ross to be denied those inviting lips, but there was much with which he could console himself.

Afterwards, they settled down into a more relaxed embrace. Her eyes closed, Bobbie had the features of an angel.

Until now, Lynette had been the pinnacle of Ross's amorous adventures, but Bobbie was something else. After their love-making, Lynette had always been edgy and borne a rather washed-out appearance, but Bobbie here looked so serene. Ross gazed into her face for a long, long time.

Ross lifted her chin with his forefinger.

"Bobbie, you're wonderful," he said.

"No I'm not," she contradicted, opening her big blue eyes wide. "You don't know me at all, Ross Clifford. If you did, you wouldn't like me much."

"Oh yes, I would."

"Ah'm not a very nice person to know, Ross."

"What makes you say that?"

"Even my own daddy doesn't think I'm nice to know."

"I can't believe that. Whyever not?"

"He doesn't like my lifestyle. He's a preacher man. I can't live up to his ideals."

"Surely he's proud of you, qualifying as a doctor, and being so beautiful."

"He says pride is a sin. He holds no store by human achievement and vanity."

"That's very sad. Bit of a tyrant, is he?"

"Oh, no. True, he lives by the Bible to the letter, but he's lovely really, and he loves me. He prays for me every day, he says. He longs for me to go back home and be with him. But I know what it would be like. He'd always be trying to get me to change - in a nice, kind way, though very persistent. But I like the good things in life - money, and having a good time."

"Who doesn't?"

"My daddy doesn't. He thinks it's sinful and I'll go to hell when I die if I don't change. He gets so upset. Whenever I'm with him he pleads with me to go back and live with him. I can't stand the pressure, I would feel so trapped if I did what he wanted."

"I'm not surprised. What about your mother?"

"She died when I was quite young."

"Oh, I'm so sorry."

"She was a lovely lady, as I recall, but she never knew me as an adult. I don't think she would have approved of me either."

"What was her name?"

"Mary."

"I'm sure she would have thought you were wonderful, just as I do."

"I'm not going to disillusion you if that's what you think, Ross. But now I need some sleep. I'm not going to get it here, am I."

She rose from the bed and Ross watched her as she dressed, almost as seductively as she had undressed.

"Have you been avoiding me these past few days?" Ross asked.

"Ah sure have, honey. I kinda figured this would happen and I wasn't certain I wanted it to."

"Any regrets now?"

"Uh-huh."

Ross took this to be a no.

He stood and took her in his arms.

"You're so beautiful, Bobbie, my darling," he said, moving his face close to hers.

"Don't go all romantic on me, Ross," she said, gently pushing him away and doing up the remaining buttons of her dress.

"I hope this isn't just a... "

She placed a finger on his lips to prevent him going further.

"I have my needs and you have yours, Ross. Let's just leave it at that. I'll see you around."

It was an attitude which Ross had always hoped his many girl friends would have adopted, but they had always been so clinging. Now that Bobbie had expressed it in words, though, Ross was not sure it was what he wanted to hear after all.

She slipped her shoes on, stepped to the door, unlocked and opened it a crack to peep out. Then, seeing no-one outside, she ventured out into the alleyway. Before closing the door behind her, she turned and blew Ross a kiss from her beautiful pursed lips and a wave of a creamy-white hand with its red-painted fingernails. Then she was gone.

Ross laid back on his bunk trying to collect answers to the multitude of questions which raced across his mind.

How had he managed that? How could his fortunes have taken such a miraculous turn? Had she just done it to clear his brain of voices? Would the voices now be gone? How many others of the ship's company had enjoyed the same treatment from their surgeon? What the devil was a doctor needed for on a ship like this anyway?

He turned to sleep without the feeling of satisfaction to which he thought he should be entitled.

But he could hear no voices now.

CHAPTER EIGHT

Next morning, Ross busied himself getting all his jobs completed so that he could relax in the afternoon. Captain Bridson was alive and well and working in his cabin.

After lunch, Ross stripped and donned his swimming trunks. Grabbing a towel and some suntan oil, he called at Bobbie's cabin. She was at her computer again.

"Fancy sunbathing on deck?" he greeted.

"No thanks, Ross. I don't sunbathe." No, she wouldn't, with that creamy-white skin. "And you shouldn't do too much either. It can be bad for you. Does that oil screen you properly? Let me see."

She studied the label carefully. She wore a freshly-laundered white dress of the same pattern as before. She must have dozens of those plain, front-buttoning dresses, Ross had never seen her in any other. Everything she wore, Ross now knew, was white. Perhaps the reason for her nickname? What would she wear in the colder weather?

He caught the whiff of perfume as he stood close to her. If she had had access to Lynette's vast wardrobe she would have looked even more sensational.

"It's not the very safest," she concluded, "but it will be okay if you don't spend more than an hour a day at it."

"Right, doctor," Ross grinned. "But you should

have some fresh air, surely."

"I like to stroll round the deck in the evening."

"Right. After dinner, then. We'll walk the deck together. Then perhaps afterwards... "

"I don't know, Ross. I have much work to do."

"What work? There's no outbreak of blackwater fever on this ship, is there? Nobody remotely ill, as far as I've seen."

Bobbie blushed, the first time he had seen her do that. It made her agonisingly kissable.

"There are always things to do," she said.

Ross looked at the computer screen. There were lots of figures under such headings as "patient number", "temperature", "pulse rate", "blood pressure", and so on. It seemed endless.

"What are all those figures?"

"Oh, just case studies."

"Are you studying for something, then? A higher qualification?"

"Sure. That's right, Ross," she smiled, the blush vanishing. "In this profession, you never stop learning."

"Sounds familiar. Right, come and find me when you want a break from all that stuff."

"Yes. Thanks, Ross. I'll do that."

The sun was still very hot as Ross stretched himself out on the monkey island, but the Atlantic breeze took away the scorching intensity there had been at anchor in the river.

Perhaps Bobbie would come and join him after all, he told himself, just as Faye had on the *Greyhound*. But his fantasies came to nothing.

He could not take his eyes off Bobbie at dinner, even though he knew it was making her feel uncomfortable. She left without finishing her dessert and Ross lowered his head as he finished his own meal.

Why was he behaving in this way? It was as if he was a silly schoolboy again.

After dinner, he went back to his cabin, resisting the temptation to knock on her door again.

He kept looking out of his window across the deck, hoping to see her taking a stroll, but by the time darkness fell she had not appeared.

He fetched himself a gin and tonic from the wardroom bar. Ian was there, knocking back a few whiskies. Ross would have liked to join him, but he did not want to miss Bobbie if she came looking for him.

He tried to relax on his bunk with the gin and his book, but he could not concentrate on the words.

Then suddenly, without warning, the sound of the singing baritone voice came through his window.

"Glorious things of thee are spoken,
Zion, city of our God.
He, whose word cannot be broken,
Formed thee for his own abode.
On the rock of ages founded,
What can shake thy sure repose?
With salvation's walls surrounded
Thou may'st smile at all thy foes."

Ross looked out into the blackness as the song continued.

"See the streams of living waters
Springing from eternal love,
Well supply thy sons and daughters,
And all fear of want remove... "

Wearily, Ross left his cabin, trudged down the stairs and walked out onto the deck, feeling his way as his eyes became accustomed to the darkness.

As he had expected, the singing had stopped and he could sense no presence of anyone else there.

He found the ventilators and edged around them, finally stopping and leaning against one.

He *must* be going mad!

He took in some deep breaths and listened to the sound of the sea breaking away from the ship's side and the muffled throb of the engine.

"Help!"

Was that a faint cry he had heard? Or just another voice in the brain? He tilted his head to one side to hear better.

"Help!"

It certainly sounded real. It came through the grille in the ventilator.

"Help!" It was louder this time but still seemed far away. "For God's sake help us!"

A second angry voice followed.

"Shut up, Zitty! Nobody can hear us."

They were not the voices he had been hearing so far.

"Help!" shouted the voice again.

"Shut up, I said." It was the second voice again.

111

"You're only making things worse."

"I'm coming," shouted Ross into the ventilator grille. There was no response.

He made his way cautiously back into the lit accommodation, down the stairs to the shelter deck, then along it aft until he came to the door labelled 'NUMBER 2 HOLD'.

It was a large steel door, with two massive lever handles, which he moved to open it. Inside, he switched on the light which lit the steep steel steps leading narrowly downwards.

Closing the door behind him, he went down the three flights to another big steel door with the same label. Opening this, he stepped onto the floor of the hold. The lights were all on but there were not many of them and they provided only a dim overall illumination.

The hold was almost empty, just four containers on the deck, spaced a few feet apart. They were chained to the deck to stop them moving about if the sea became rough.

Ross closed the door behind him and moved closer to the nearest container. A smell of... what?... animals?... entered his nostrils and, sure enough, he noticed the bars of grilles at three different levels in the sides of the containers.

Cautiously, he approached one and moved up to one of the grilles to peer in. The hold lights could not penetrate the interior more than a few inches.

He put his face up to the grille.

"Aaah!"

Ross jumped back as a black face was thrust at him from the other side of the grille. The whites of the eyes caught the beam from the lights.

It was a human face. African. There was a rattling of chains from inside.

"Who are you?" gasped Ross.

The African made some angry-sounding utterance in a language he could not understand.

"Hey, you! Over here!" The man's voice came from another of the containers behind Ross.

Ross turned and stepped nervously towards it.

A white hand clasped one of the bars as Ross peered in to see the pasty face of a man of about thirty.

"Who are you?" repeated Ross to the new face.

"I'm Brian Lapworth from England," said the face. "There's a torch on the wall over there."

Ross turned his eyes towards the door to see the large rubber torch clipped to the bulkhead alongside the door. He walked across and unclipped it. Returning to the container, he switched it on and shone it through the bars.

He took a rough estimate of the number of the men inside, all white and mostly quite young - some of them only boys, the man Brian seemed the oldest. They were on two levels, about twenty on the floor and about half that number on a shelf which ran all round the steel box. All were dressed in white overalls and were chained by the wrist to the side walls.

"So who are you?" asked the spokesman called Brian.

"I'm the radio officer."

"Radio officer? Where's Owen?"

"Owen? The previous radio officer? He's dead, I'm afraid."

"Shit!" This came from a different voice from deep within. "The bastards!"

"What's going on?" asked Ross. "Why are you all here?"

"That's what we'd like to know," spoke a third voice. "Don't you?"

"No."

"Neither did Owen," said Brian. "He stumbled on us just like you did. He was going to radio for help. That was weeks ago."

"I'm afraid he committed suicide. Jumped over the side," said Ross.

"Jumped, my arse!" said the second voice.

"So when did you come here?" asked Brian.

"A few days ago. In Sierra Leone."

"That's where those poor sods came on board." Brian nodded towards the container where Ross had seen the African face. "We've been here weeks longer. We were picked up in England."

"Picked up?"

"By some phoney police."

"All of you? Together?"

"No. In ones and twos. We were moved from van to lorry and finally onto this ship. The people here gave us these overalls. They feed us and hose us down occasionally, but they won't tell us anything."

"I'm afraid I can't enlighten you either. I had no idea," said Ross.

"You must know where we're going."

"Yes, of course. Charleston, South Carolina."

"America?" Brian's voice rose in disbelief. "That's the last place I thought they'd be taking us." Then, after a long pause: "Unless they're just going to bring on some more there before moving on."

"We go back to Liverpool after that," said Ross.

"So it must be America. There'd be no point in keeping us here just to take us back home."

Ross tried desperately to collect his thoughts.

"Have you no idea at all why you're here?" he asked.

"Not a clue. I told you."

"You're all British men - and boys?"

"Yes. They're from Sierra Leone over there. And the women are in the other two containers."

"Women?"

"Yes. Some from the U.K. in one, some from Sierra Leone in the other. They've segregated us by sex and country of origin."

"Have any of you been singing hymns?"

"Hymns?" Brian took a hard look at Ross. "No. We've shouted out many times, especially in the first few days, but we've not been reduced to singing *Nearer My God to Thee* or anything like that. This ship isn't called the *Titanic*, is it?"

"It's the *Duke of Argyll.*"

"Yes. I know that much. Just joking, but it's not

really funny. Can you radio for help?"

"I suppose so, yes," said Ross hesitatingly, thinking of the ill-fated Owen.

"Then bloody well get on with it," came another voice from the interior.

"Well, I... " began Ross, but he was interrupted by a clanking noise from the direction of the door. He saw the lever handles moving. Quickly, he switched off the torch and darted behind one of the other containers.

Peering through the bars of the prisons, Ross saw two of the engineers enter - the third and fourth. They were giggling and obviously rather drunk. They each carried a huge spanner.

The third, Jimmy Morgan, also carried a bunch of keys. They made their way to the far container and looked in.

"Can't see very well," said the fourth, Bob Cropper. He looked towards the door. "Somebody's taken the torch away."

"Open the door," said Morgan.

The key grated in the lock, the levers were swung out and the massive doors opened on creaking hinges. The two looked inside.

"I don't like yours," sniggered Cropper.

"That's the one," said Morgan. "Unlock her."

The two emerged from the container dragging a white woman with long black hair, dressed just like the men, in overalls, which Morgan began to unbutton. The woman pulled away.

"Hold still, darlin'," Cropper said, "unless you

want a smack with this." He brandished one of the spanners above her head.

They manhandled her to a darkened corner and Ross heard some shuffling noises.

"Help me, you bastard!" she shouted.

Ross knew the cry was directed at himself, but what could he do with one rubber torch against two men with weighty spanners?

"Nobody's goin' to help you, darlin'. You might as well lie back and enjoy it."

Hissing noises emerged from the open women's container, followed by the noisy rattling of chains from all the containers and a few shouts of "Bastards!"

"Be patient, darlins. Your turns will come."

The two men laughed.

The woman cried out and this was followed by some grunting noises.

Ross gripped the torch tightly, but did not move.

Finally, Morgan emerged into the light, zipping himself up.

"Your turn," he said to his companion.

"I don't want that one," was Cropper's reply.

"Oh, got your eye on something else, have you? Let's get this one back, then."

They pulled the woman back into the light and threw the overalls back at her. Sullenly, she clothed herself and was led back into the container. Inside were sounds of chains being rattled.

"I want one of the other lot," said Cropper as they re-emerged.

117

"Oh, yeah? A wild one, eh? Let's lock this door first, then."

The door of the container was barred and locked, then the two men walked towards the container behind which Ross crouched.

He gripped his torch tightly as they opened the door of the container. Ross could just see the smirks on their faces as they peered inside.

"That young one." Cropper pointed a finger.

A slight, cringing figure in overalls was pulled out into the light. It was a black girl. Her would-be molester put his finger beneath her chin and lifted her head.

Ross suppressed a gasp. The young girl had dimpled cheeks and sparkling, popping eyes. Yehu! Unmistakable.

While Morgan held a spanner over her head, Cropper slowly unbuttoned her overalls and pushed his hands inside. She gave a little cry.

Ross was shaking. Was it fear or rage? Or something else? He gripped the torch in anguish. Surely he was not going to let this happen to Yema's daughter - Yema who had nursed him back to health and been such a great friend until her tragedy?

Yet he remained transfixed. As the overalls fell from Yehu's shoulders, leaving her naked and weeping, he raised the torch but his feet would not move from the spot.

Yehu was pushed to the deck. It was now or never. Cropper unzipped himself. Ross's fingernails bit into the palm of his left hand, but he still made no move.

Then the noise of the door to the hold opening again turned all heads. The levers moved and the door opened. Into the hold stepped a figure in white.

"What gives here?" It was Bobbie.

"Well, look who it is," sneered Cropper as he stood over Yehu. "It's the virgin surgeon."

"What are you doing to that girl?"

"What's it look like, darlin'? D'you want some too?" Cropper turned towards Bobbie, raised his spanner and shook his hips in a provocative gesture.

Bobbie stepped towards him. Slowly, she began unbuttoning her dress from the top, revealing the lacy white bra beneath.

"Zow-ee!" called the man she faced. "She does want some. Come here then, darlin'."

Ross's mouth hung open.

Bobbie's hand reached inside her dress under her armpit, and produced a small hand gun which she pointed at the engineer.

"Drop that wrench, you ass-hole," she spat.

Cropper did as he was told.

"You too," Bobbie demanded, turning the gun towards Morgan, who also obeyed instantly.

"Now, give that girl her clothes and put her back where you found her."

"The bastards did it to me first, Miss Arthur," came a voice from the white women's container as Yehu was led back into her own. Bobbie looked briefly in the direction of the voice but said nothing.

She turned back towards the two engineers after

they had finished locking Yehu back into her container.

"Where did you get those keys?"

"From the mate's cabin, while he was on watch," said Morgan.

"All right, drop 'em!"

Morgan looked at her aghast.

"The keys, you fool," she said.

Morgan let the keys clatter to the deck with some slight look of relief on his face. "Now, git out of here," she ordered. "Go straight to the captain's cabin. I'll be up directly."

The two men left. Bobbie picked up the keys and the spanners and looked carefully around the hold before following them out and closing the door behind her.

For a few moments there was a hush in the hold. Ross moved round to look in through the bars at Yehu, who was shaking.

"Are you all right, Yehu?" he asked.

She looked up in amazement.

"Uncle Ross!" she cried. "Is it really you?"

"It's a long story, Yehu. I'll tell you some day."

"Can you get us out?"

"I will. I promise."

"Like you stopped those two bastards, eh?" called the familiar voice from the white women's cage. "We won't hold our breath."

Ross stepped across to face his accuser through the bars.

"Look, I'm sorry. But there were two of them and they carried those great spanners."

"You could have done *something*. Or did you enjoy watching, you pervert?"

"Shut up, Rachel." The new voice came from the other side of the same prison. "I think he's on our side. Come over here, *Uncle* Ross."

Ross walked round to the other side of the container and looked in at a young girl with cropped red hair and wearing the usual overalls which had been unbuttoned to the waist, revealing enough to show she too had nothing on underneath.

"Hi. I'm Sandra. If you can get us out of here, hunk, I'll give you the time of your life. Okay?"

"Look, I'll do what I can," said Ross, "but I've got to be careful. It won't do you any good if I end up the same way as Owen. First of all, what can you tell me about all this? You say you have no idea why you're here."

"No," said Sandra. "We'd come round to thinking we were heading for the Middle East - prostitution, that sort of thing."

"And all these men?"

"Well, there could be a demand for them too. But if it's the U.S.A...."

"There was another rumour about Antigua," said Ross, "but only a rumour."

"That's a holiday island, isn't it?"

"Right."

"You think we might be some sort of attraction for *tourists*?"

"I've no idea. I'll find out."

121

"Never mind that." It was Brian from the men's container. "Just send out a call for help."

Ross walked back to face Brian again.

"I think I know a way, but as I said I'll have to be careful. The Old Man won't let me transmit anything without his permission."

"Do it when he's in bed, then."

"There's always somebody around, on watch on the bridge nearby. I don't know who I can trust yet. But leave it to me. You must be patient."

"Patient?!"

"Look, we're in mid-Atlantic. We're not going to reach anywhere for at least a week. It will be easier when we get nearer the U.S. coastguard ships."

"I see."

"You know the girl who came in and took those characters away?"

"She's the ship's doctor, Miss Arthur. She's one of them but she looks after us, seeing that we're well fed. Before we came on this ship we had only rice and bananas. We were starving. But she's very fussy about us. She has us - and these containers - hosed down every few days. She takes our temperatures, pulses, blood pressures and so on regularly. She's always down here."

"On her own?"

"Not as a rule. Usually there are a few crew members with her. They've got guns - pistols. I've never seen her with a gun before. She tells them what to do with us. Sometimes the captain comes down too, to see what's going on. They must all have been and had a look

122

at us at some time or other. You must be the only one who didn't know about us."

"And have any of them done *that* sort of thing before?"

"No. They've not abused any of us till now, apart from keeping us locked up here."

"Right. Carry on as if nothing has happened. You might not see me for some time, but don't worry. I'll do whatever's necessary."

"That's what Owen said."

"Yes. Well, I've got a bit more forewarning."

"Okay. Thanks. Be careful, but for God's sake get help as soon as you can."

"Right. Of course. By the way, are you sure nobody down here has been singing hymns?"

"No. Why all this thing about hymns? Are they religious nutters? Some kind of weird cult?"

"I don't know. I don't think so, though maybe one of them is."

"Shit!" shrieked a voice from behind Brian.

"Keep calm," said Ross, "I'm going off now."

"Good luck," said Brian.

A rattling of chains seemed to give approval to what had been said.

Ross took a last look into the African women's container.

"I'll get you back to your mother, Yehu. Don't worry."

The dimpled smile he received in reply was weak but full of hope. He replaced the torch, turned and strode grimly out of the hold, up the steps and out into the fresh but warm night air of the shelter deck. He made straight for the wardroom, where he poured himself a quadruple gin and tonic, then carried it back up to his cabin, where he sat down heavily on his bunk and took a big gulp.

Countless dilemmas seemed to become all jumbled in his brain. How should he radio for help? What could he do about Bobbie? Should he confide in Ian? How could he get Yehu back to her mother? Could he avoid the same fate as Owen? Was he an unwitting partner in the activities of some religious cult? Did he really have the balls to do anything about it at ? Did the mate always wear his monocle over the same eye?

God! What was he thinking? How could he dream of being so flippant?

He downed the rest of his drink and then as he lay thrashing about on his bed in anguish, the sound of the singing voice entered through the window. He froze and listened.

> *"When the poor pris'ner through a grate*
> *Sees others walk at large.*
> *How does he mourn his lonely state,*
> *And long for a discharge!*
> *Thus I, confined in unbelief,*
> *My loss of freedom mourn;*
> *And spend my hours in fruitless grief,*
> *Until my Lord return.*
>
> *The beam of day, which pierces through*
> *The gloom in which I dwell,*

124

Only discloses to my view
The horrors of my cell."

Ross rose and moved to the window, lowered the shutter and peered out into the blackness. It was not in his head. It was a real voice. A man's voice. Newton's. Whoever *he* was.

"But now my joys are all cut off,
In prison I am cast;
And Satan with a cruel scoff
Says Where's your God at last?"

"SHARRAP!" yelled Ross. But the singing continued without pause.

"Dear Saviour, for thy mercy's sake,
My strong, my only plea,
These gates and bars and pieces break,
And let the pris'ner free!"

Ross raised the shutter, before knocking back the drink, undressing and getting into his bunk.

He covered his head with the bedclothes to shut out the sound. The problems could wait until morning.

Ross did not sleep straight away, however. It wasn't the sound of the singing - that stopped within a minute or so. It wasn't the problems he faced either - they seemed so insurmountable that he couldn't even begin to look for solutions until he had slept and re-collected his thoughts in the cold light of day.

No, it was the situation with the British captives. What they had said somehow didn't quite ring true. Captured in ones and twos by bogus policemen? There must have been forty or fifty of them. How could so many disappear without being noticed by the police or the press or their loved ones?

Okay, people disappear all the time, he tried to reason - most simply run away from problems or relationships and don't want to be found, not unlike his own situation.   But this was a sizeable number, presumably in a fairly short space of time.

Someone must have missed them and reported the fact to the police.   Someone must surely have known where these people were at the time of their abduction. He had not heard anything about scores of missing persons back home, but then he was not one for keeping up with the news.

With these questions still unanswered running around in his brain, Ross finally succumbed to sleep.

CHAPTER NINE

At ten a.m. on the twentysixth of May, Justin was arrested for the seventeenth time for car theft. At noon on the same day, he was allowed to leave the police station with yet another caution. He turned in the doorway to the W.P.C. who had arrested him. The smirk on his face gave the lie to his blonde-haired, choirboy appearance.

"See you, then, won't I?"

"Make the most of it, Justin," replied the W.P.C. without much conviction, "you'll soon be old enough. British justice will catch up with you before long."

Justin extended his right arm and poked his middle finger skyward to show his contempt for the Greater Manchester police in general and this W.P.C. in particular.

After the door had swung closed behind him, he saw Darren waiting, sitting on a wall, picking his nose and swinging his legs. He gave Justin a faint smile and jumped down in silent greeting. The pair ambled off down the street, shoulders hunched.

"Got the tools, have you?"

"Yeah." Darren was a lad of few words.

After raiding the fridge, they spent all afternoon at Darren's playing scalectrix. Darren's Mum gave them tea, then they set off around the streets, Darren clutching a plastic bag. It was seven in the evening when they spotted the black Golf GTI with no steering wheel clamp. They gave it a few shoves - no alarm sounded.

Darren did his screwdriver job on the driver's door and Justin leapt into the seat, releasing the bonnet catch for Darren to do the hot wiring. Then Justin wrenched the steering lock.

The engine chattered into life, then screamed, the rev counter flicking round violently as Justin stabbed on the accelerator pedal, unlocking the passenger door at the same time.

Darren jumped in and they were away.

A pensioner walking his little dog was startled by the squeal of the tyres, then glowered at the car as it sped away. The terrier barked an endorsement of his master's disgust.

Over the crossroads and round the bend roared the Golf. A car with a L plates was coming from the opposite direction. Justin drove straight at it, only swerving at the last second. They rocked with laughter on seeing the young girl driver's shocked face and the indignation of the bespectacled driving instructor.

Justin jumped the red at the junction and swerved left, clipping the side of a Sierra as he did so.

Darren gripped the seat and grinned. They were heading for their favourite street, a wide tree-lined avenue where rich folk lived, where the council hadn't yet got around to putting humps across the road. Justin and Darren were well known to the residents here, who were powerless to prevent their fun, which added to the thrill.

A sharp right took them into it. The Golf lurched wildly. Justin gave it lots of wellie and they touched ninety down the long straight. He eased off only slightly to take the long left-hand bend.

"Shit!" yelled Justin, as an old blue Transit van moved out from the side of the road right into their path. Justin stood on the brakes. A burning smell quickly followed the screech and blue smoke wisped up from the front corners of the car. He wrenched the wheel to the right to avoid a head-on into the back of the Transit, crunching the offside wing into the side of a Jaguar.

Water spurted from the front of the Golf. At least it had been a glancing blow and both boys were all right. They quickly slipped off their seatbelts. Justin leapt out but Darren couldn't open his door.

Justin made to run off, but two enormous policemen suddenly appeared from behind the Transit and pinned him by the arms.

"You're nicked!" Justin heard as he felt the cuffs bite into his wrists.

"Ouch! Careful! I'll have you for using unnecessary force, won't I?" Justin knew his rights.

"Shut up, you little cretin," growled the officer and smacked his open hand hard across Justin's ear.

"Ow! You saw that, didn't you?" Justin demanded of his friend as the other officer pulled Darren from the car. Darren nodded vigorously. "Right, copper. Got a good lawyer, have you?"

The only reply Justin received this time was a punch in the face. He grunted in pain, then felt the blood trickling down over his lips. He didn't recognise this officer, who had a fat face with small, piggy eyes, and he decided it would be better to keep quiet until they reached the nick.

The two were led to the back of the Transit, where Darren's equally large captor opened the doors. Justin didn't recognise this one either, who leered at him from behind a greying beard.

By this time a few people had gathered round.

"'Bout time, too!" yelled a middle-aged, woolly-jumpered man. "Give the little bleeders a good thrashing this time."

"Lock 'em up and throw away the key," voiced an otherwise genteel-looking elderly lady.

"My car!" howled an overweight young man. "I'll want a report from you two for the insurance."

"Call in at the station tomorrow, sir," replied Darren's escort as the youths were shoved into the back of the van. Their handcuffs were snapped onto angle-iron fitted inside the walls of the van - Justin on one side, Darren on the other. Then the doors were slammed, the officers got in the front and the van was driven off.

Justin managed to wipe a sleeve across his bleeding nose and cut lip. He frowned. He had travelled in many police cars and vans, but this one was different. It was more like a builder's van than a police vehicle. He had heard about police brutality but had never experienced it himself before. The officers of his acquaintance, male and female, had always been very careful.

The van seemed to be going a very long way and quite fast, as if they were on the motorway. But that would mean they were leaving town. The windows in the back doors were too high to see through except to view the sky. Justin looked in vain for some crack in the van sides through which he might peep.

There was a bulkhead between them and the policemen in the front, with a window in the middle of it. Justin yelled at the window.

"Hey! Where're you taking us?"

The fat face with the small, piggy eyes appeared at the window. The officer just grinned at Justin and waved at him as if in goodbye. Then the face turned away again.

"I don't like the look of this," Justin pronounced.

"I want to go home," said Darren bleakly, "I'm hungry."

Then the hissing noise started. At first Justin thought they might have a puncture and his spirits rose briefly. But the van continued its journey at full speed and the ride was no bumpier.

The hissing noise continued.

Darren's head fell down onto his chest.

Justin's eyelids drooped and he could not lift them again.

. . . .

The stolen Volvo estate swept smoothly through the town and out towards the suburbs, only slightly above the speed limit so as not to attract attention.

The four members of the Pound Lane gang - Josh, Zitty, Mike and Ben, all in their early twenties - were silent.

It was two o'clock on the morning of May the

twentyeighth and the streets were deserted.

Josh steered the car into a small service road with shops all down one side and car parking opposite. The off-licence was in complete darkness. Josh turned and parked across the road opposite the doorway, the rear of the Volvo lined up towards the shop door. There were still no barriers in front of the shop. Would they never learn? The Pound Lane gang had done the place twice themselves in the last six months, and they weren't the only ones. It had been done so many times the owners could no longer buy insurance.

"Let's get goin', then." Ben always made the final decision.

They pulled the hoods over their heads, leaving only slits for eyes, nose and mouth, and each gripped a sack and a baseball bat tightly.

Josh revved the Volvo, slammed it into reverse and let out the clutch. The car shot backwards, tyres smoking, and smashed easily through the door, splintering the woodwork and showering the inside of the shop with broken glass.

Josh left the engine running. They all jumped out.

"Just fags and spirits, remember," called Ben.

Zitty and Mike ran along the shelves of spirits, clanking bottles into their sacks, while Josh and Ben made to climb over the counter for the cigarettes.

A fat face with small, piggy eyes shot up from behind the counter in front of them and grinned. Josh started to swing his club, but the rest of the big man's body rose before their eyes. Then the two barrels of the shotgun emerged.

Ben's mind struggled to reconcile police uniforms with shotguns, then he saw the flame from one of the barrels a split-second before the explosion deafened him. A hundred bottles on the shelves behind Mike and Zitty splintered into a sparkling liquorfall.

Smoke and a smell of scorching issued from Josh's hood as he dropped heavily onto his bottom on the floor, like a baby failing in its first attempt at walking.

Climbing over the counter, the policeman pulled off Josh's hood, revealing a bewildered and colour-drained but unscratched face.

Ben froze as the gun pointed at himself, he presumed with one barrel still loaded.

A second officer, big again, with a greying beard, came in from a side door carrying another shotgun, aimed at Mike and Zitty, who had adopted freeze-frame poses.

Mike dropped a bottle onto the floor. Broken glass shattered around his feet and the whisky flowed around his and Zitty's trainers.

"Over the road and into the back of the blue Transit," ordered the bearded one, pulling off their hoods and kicking the baseball bats aside. "Move it!"

Manhandled into the back of the van, they were handcuffed to angle-iron fixed to the inner walls.

"Not a sound," commanded the fat-faced one as he slammed the doors, leaving them in the pitch dark.

The van roared into life and sped off, rocking the members of the Pound Lane gang to and fro as corners were negotiated.

Numbed into silence by the events of the past five minutes, none of them dared utter a word, even when the hissing noise started.

. . . .

They had been working late at the office. Really they had! It was the last day of May and the records had to be bang up to date for the first-of-the-month meeting the next day. Brian had phoned his wife, even though she would have known it was on the cards he'd be working late, and Rachel had phoned her husband - he would not need to come for her as Brian would bring her home. It was a monthly routine - everyone in the office knew they did it, yet their spouses had never suspected.

Brian's gaze moved from the VDU screen to Rachel's long, black hair, then down to her slender legs. Her neat black skirt was not only short, it was drawn up high as she sat at her desk. Her bra could be seen beneath her thin white blouse.

It wouldn't be long now if they hurried. He would have taken her here on the office carpet - he had suggested it more than once before - but she worried about the security officers doing their rounds.

She noticed his stare, pouted back at him and ran her tongue provocatively over her lips.

He turned back to the VDU and pummelled the keyboard as fast as he could. Rachel attacked her word processor with a renewed frenzy.

By five to ten they had finished and by ten o'clock were on the road. It was pitch dark as the car edged its way down the little lane and onto the grass verge at their usual spot. They leapt out, re-entered the rear of the car and tumbled onto the back seat.

The windows quickly steamed up as they pulled at each other's clothes. Brian ran his hands up Rachel's long, lovely legs, while she pulled off his shirt and began digging her nails into his back.

They failed to notice the other vehicle glide noiselessly to a stop on the grass behind them, its engine cut and its lights extinguished.

The first they heard was a violent banging on the windows. Frantically, they tried to pull their clothes back on but they hadn't achieved very much in that direction when the rear doors were opened and powerful torches shone at them from both sides.

"'Ello, 'ello, 'ello. What's all this, then?"

The policemen's faces were illuminated by each other's torches. It was the one with the fat face and small, piggy eyes who spoke the time-worn phrases with such heavy sarcasm.

"Looks like an act of gross indecency to me," declared the one with the greying beard as he leered at Rachel's state of undress. "Out of the car, both of you."

Brian was pushed round the back of a van, parked behind his own car, where he was shoved in through the back doors and handcuffed to some angle-iron attached to the inner wall.

"Hey! This is a bit over the top, isn't it?"

"Shut up," spat the bearded one and slammed the doors, leaving Brian alone in the dark.

He strained his ears to try and hear what was going on outside. There were a few bumps against the side of the van.

"No!" It was Rachel's voice. "You bastards!"

The bumpings went on for a long time, ceasing only once, for a few brief moments. Then suddenly they stopped and he heard Rachel's voice again.

"Does this mean you're going to let me go now?"

Both men laughed. Then the van doors opened again and Rachel was bundled in and handcuffed just like himself on the other side of the van. In the few seconds of torchlight during this, Brian saw she was almost naked, just clinging to the remains of her torn and dirty blouse and skirt. Then the doors were slammed again and they were both in darkness.

"Bastards!" she snarled. "Now I know why they're called pigs."

"I can't believe policemen are doing this," said Brian as the van sped off, rocking them to and fro.

"You're right. I don't think they're real police."

"Then who?"

"You tell me."

A long silence followed. Soon the van appeared to be on a smooth road and travelling at high speed.

"What's that?" cried Brian suddenly.

"What?"

"That noise."

"What noise?"

"Listen."

"That hissing noise?"

136

"Yes. What is it?"

"I don't know."

Brian yawned.

"Did they hurt you?"

"What do you care?" Rachel spoke the words drowsily. "It took you long enough to ask."

Nothing more was said in the back of the blue Transit van as it made rapid progress northwards along the M6 motorway.

. . . .

Sandra eyed the front of the small terraced house. It was a dead giveaway - ugly big nineteen-thirties style statuette of Pan in the window in front of the grey lace curtains, peeling paint on the door, rotting windowsills, even the back of an old dressing table showing at the bedroom window. Then there was the best indication of all - a small chalk mark of an arrow on the gatepost, which Sandra's sisterhood used to identify the homes of elderly people living alone.

She pressed the doorbell, leaving her finger on the button for an extended period. The hand concealed behind the seat of her jeans held a plastic bucket.

At last the door was opened slightly, on the security chain, and a thin short, elderly lady peered out suspiciously at the young girl with the cropped red hair.

"I'm so sorry to bother you," said Sandra, using her cultured, pleading voice, "but my car has overheated and I need to top up the radiator." She produced the bucket, tilting her head prettily. "Would you mind terribly

137

filling this with water?"

After a long pause, the old lady slowly slipped off the chain, opened the door wider and reached out a wrinkled hand to take the bucket.

Sandra put her shoulder to the door and barged in, pushing the old lady against the wall inside her hall, then slammed the door shut behind her.

"Right, gran. Where's the money?"

"Oh! I... I... don't keep any... money in the... house," whimpered the old lady.

"Don't give me that crap." Sandra shook the bucket very close to the woman's grey face. "Get into your living room, we'll start there."

Sandra pushed the old lady along as she shuffled through a door into a room which seemed untouched since the second world war, then shoved her down onto the floral-patterned sofa.

Sandra gave a gasp as the huge figure of a policeman rose from behind the sofa, placing large, rough hands on the antimacassar. He spoke gently through a greying beard.

"Well, well, well. Is this your social worker then, Mrs Fairbrass?"

The old lady cackled.

Sandra turned to run, but another large officer with a fat face and small, piggy eyes blocked the doorway.

"Put that bucket down, you slut. You're coming with us."

At the end of what seemed about an hour-long journey in the back of the van, handcuffed to angle-iron on the side, Sandra suddenly realised they had stopped.

The back doors were opened, her two captors released her handcuffs and pulled her out.

She looked around. They had arrived in the untidy yard of an old farmhouse, confirming her suspicions that these cops were not kosher. A large articulated van was parked nearby and it was to the back of this that Sandra was led.

The two men opened the huge steel door at the back of the truck and the bearded one pulled out some steps up to it. Sandra was pushed inside, where thirty or more gaunt faces, mostly of teenagers or twenty-somethings all handcuffed to the walls, peered up at her, curious but unsurprised.

Sandra was similarly clamped and sat down heavily on the steel floor next to a girl who wore what had been a smart skirt and blouse but was now torn and dirty.

The two men left without a word and closed the door with heavy clanking noises.

Light was still able to penetrate the steel prison through gratings at the very top of the walls. The other occupants stared silently at the newcomer.

"What is this?" Sandra asked of her nearest neighbour.

Rachel shrugged.

"We hoped you could tell us," she replied. "We hope every new body who's pushed in here can tell us something, but nobody can."

"They're bloody nutters," offered Zitty in a high-pitched, frenetic voice.

"Ex coppers, I reckon," volunteered Justin, "trying to get their own back on us."

"Vigilantes," declared Ben. "Anti-crime fanatics. They don't know what it's like to have nothin'. They'd rather kill us than share their things with anybody."

"They're not vigilantes," said Rachel emphatically. "We weren't committing any crime when they picked us up. We'd only stopped the car to have a ... to have a talk."

Brian shuffled his feet.

"We wasn't doing anything wrong either," a boy of about eleven piped up. "We was only playing in the wood instead of going to school."

The long silence which followed was broken by Brian.

"The only connection I can see is that we were all in places where no-one knew we were.

"Right," said Ben. "And no-one would know where to start lookin' for us."

"Shit!" squealed Zitty.

"Can't we all shout for help together?" suggested Sandra.

"Have you seen where we are?" wailed Zitty. "Miles from any-bloody-where."

"They'd only turn the gas on," said Darren resignedly.

"Gas?" Sandra's experience was not quite the same as the others'.

"To knock us out," explained Rachel. "Didn't you get any?"

"No."

Silence descended on the group as each became absorbed in confused thought.

Darren wondered when the next lot of food would be brought, though he hoped it wouldn't be bread and bananas again.

CHAPTER TEN

John Newton sat grim-faced at the little table in his cabin beneath the poop deck. In front of him was his bible, open at the book of Galatians, chapter five. Though alone, he read aloud from verse nineteen.

"Now the works of the flesh are manifest, which are these: adultery, fornication, uncleanness, lasciviousness."

He closed the book and gazed out of the stern window. The sea was glassy smooth, with barely a ripple to indicate any wake. There was hardly a creak from the ship's timbers.

Checking briefly his general appearance - the shiny buckles of his shoes, the buttons of his waistcoat and jacket - he picked up his navy blue tricorn hat with its white beading around the edge and placed it firmly on his head before rising. For reassurance, he touched the handle of the cutlass at his side and that of the pistol in his belt before stooping to pass through the door. At the age of only twentyfive, he had to be sure to preserve his aura of authority over the many older men under his command.

He mounted the wooden steps and emerged onto the deck, where the ship's company had assembled and were awaiting his arrival. Above them, the sails hung limp in the awful stillness.

Regarding the two men before him, their feet chained together and hands bound with rope, he spoke, his words directed towards the wretched pair yet loud enough to be heard by every member of the crew.

"Gentlemen - if indeed you are now entitled to the name - you are guilty of the most lewd and brutish crime of fornication, namely the lying, without even their permission, with female slaves numbers eightyone and ninetyfive. We are all aware that such flagrant, wanton rudeness is tolerated - even encouraged - in many of the ships engaged in this trade. Those responsible for allowing such debauchery will be judged, never fear. But equally, you must by now be aware that I do not permit any such barbaric behaviour aboard my ship, and that the punishment for these crimes must be of the utmost severity."

One of the two miscreants began to shake.

"Your punishment, gentlemen, is to be three dozen stripes apiece. Mister Hallin! Prepare to administer my instruction."

The bo's'n had no need to issue verbal orders. At a wave of his hand, six sailors removed the shirts from the two prisoners, led them to the ship's side and tied their hands high up in the shrouds, so that their bare backs faced inboard. Two other sailors stepped forward brandishing cat o' nine tails.

"Carry on, Mister Hallin," commanded the captain.

"ONE!" shouted the bo's'n. The barbed whips fell.

"TWO!"

At the count of five, the red weals began to ooze blood.

"SIX!"

At the count of eight, one of the men uttered a cry, the other gritting his teeth defiantly. At ten, the first man screamed and the other began to half-grunt, half-sob.

"ELEVEN!"

The backs of the men were now a bloody mess.

"TWELVE!"

"STOP!" called Newton.

The whips were held down at the sailors' sides.

"Salt water!" ordered the master.

Two further sailors dashed the contents of their buckets across the backs of the offenders.

"Cut them down."

The bo's'n himself freed their arms from the shrouds.

"Turn to face the captain!" he shouted.

"Remember this day you have received mercy," declared Newton, "mercy you did not show to those unfortunate creatures below. But God has been merciful to me, so now I am merciful to you. Not one of us deserves mercy. I myself was steeped in sin until, by the Lord's amazing grace, I was set free. You also can be freed from sin by acknowledging the Lord Jesus Christ as your Saviour from the fires of hell. Otherwise, be sure that the wages of sin is death."

The relieved but defiant features of the two men confirmed to Newton that his words once again fell on deaf ears. But he was a patient man, humbled by past experiences. He directed his next pronouncements to the whole of the ship's company.

"Gentlemen, do not for one moment think that I shall be as merciful with anyone else who commits such a vile crime. I know you must be tempted also. To my shame, I too from time to time am tempted by the carnal lusts of my old human nature. Although I love my dear wife more than life itself, during these long voyages the presence of women slaves - all of them helpless and some of them even willing - causes diabolical stirrings in my loins. But we are not barbarians. We have a responsibility to the poor heathen whom God has entrusted to our care.

"For your edification, I will repeat advice which I have given you many times before. I find it beneficial in the curbing of the lusts of the flesh, to abstain from flesh itself. That is to say, I refrain from the eating of meat while I am apart from my dear wife. Also, I drink only water. I believe my temptation would be the greater if I were to drink tankards of nasty flip, as some of you are in the habit of doing. I shall not force you to do these things, God has given you free will, but I pray you will take this advice for the sake of your immortal souls."

The faint smirks on the faces of many of the sailors told Newton his pearls of wisdom were once more cast before swine.

"In our services on the sabbath we shall pray earnestly for a favourable wind to speed us on our voyage.

"I exhort you to learn the words of the new hymn I taught you while we were on the coast. Mister Gallagher has perfected the tune on his fiddle. If our praise and worship is pleasing to God, I am certain his grace and favour will be ours.

"Now, Mister Couture, I believe the tea-kettle is boiling. After our refreshment, Mister Hamilton will supervise the exercise, and washing of the men slaves on deck. Only a dozen at a time, if you please, and ensure their irons are secure."

"Aye-aye, sir," the third mate responded.

"Now the ship's company is dismissed."

The sailors hurried off below. Newton turned to his surgeon.

"Will you take tea with me in my room, Mister Arthur?"

"Aye, sir. Gladly." The captain's requests were thinly-veiled orders, but the surgeon was a willing and agreeable confidant.

As they sat in the cabin, sipping from the steaming mugs, Robert Arthur waited for his commander to lead the conversation.

"A miserable business, Mister Arthur," declared Newton.

"Aye, sir."

"I am oft in despair over the souls of the people in my charge."

"Only a few will enter the narrow gate, as the Good Lord said, sir."

"I fear that is the case among our own company, Robert."

"Aye, sir."

"I have several times had a vision."

146

"Sir?"

"As I take my stroll in the evening, I sometimes see a huge iron structure, straddling the main deck and extending over the sides of the ship. There are windows all around it and a chimney on top, belching smoke. Blazing light issues from those windows, but the people within are not yet consumed by the fire. No! They are carousing and indulging in all manner of evils."

The surgeon's eyebrows raised as his captain continued.

"'Tis the fiery furnace, Robert. Aboard my ship. What does it mean?"

"A warning, sir?"

"Aye. But of what? I do my best for our people and for the slaves, Robert. You'll bear witness to that."

"Aye, sir."

"This is the line of life Divine Providence has given us. I find the punishments and the chains and shackles disagreeable, but I hope I discharge the duties God has entrusted to me with as much humanity as possible."

"You do, sir. You need have no fears of Judgment upon that score. And your gift for hymn-writing must mean you have received God's blessing."

"Aye, Robert. I am ever thankful to the Almighty for the ability to praise Him in song. I shall allow you to share one of my secrets, Robert."

"Sir?"

"At present, all these songs are in my head and scribbled on scraps of paper for our people on board here to sing as best they are able. But, one day, I pray that they will be published in an hymnal for all of God's children to sing. What do you think of that?"

"I am convinced you will achieve that worthy ambition, sir."

"Aye. It is one of my heart's desires to write a song for every passage of God's word."

"That would be an enormous task, sir."

"Aye, Robert, so it would. I pray for the Lord to send someone to assist me. Someone with a poetic soul and Christian sensibilities. Perchance you would... ?"

"Oh, no, sir. Not I. I have no gift in that regard."

"Ah."

The pair turned to look out of the stern window in a few moments of silence.

"Still no sign of a blow, sir," said Arthur.

"No," Newton agreed. "Yet by my reckoning, we are ten dozen leagues farther west than we were yesterday."

The surgeon's eyebrows raised again.

"Is that possible, sir?"

"I have never experienced a current so strong in any waters, Robert. 'Tis God's hand at work... "

"Aye, sir."

"... or my observations are in error."

It was not a suggestion the surgeon could have dared make himself, even if he had wanted to.

"We shall have to see what the noon reckoning brings today. Thank you for your company, Mister Arthur. You have been a great comfort to me this voyage, especially since poor Mister Bridson passed on."

"Thank you, sir."

"I shall now take the air on deck."

The two men rose.

"I shall go and assist Mister Hamilton," said Arthur.

As the surgeon left, Newton lifted the lid of his sea chest and removed a sheet of paper bearing the words of his latest sacrifice of worship.

Mounting the steps to the poop deck, he glanced with approval towards the main deck, where his third mate and surgeon were supervising the washing and shaving of a dozen sullen-faced man-slaves, chained by their feet to the iron rails along the centre of the deck.

Staying well back from these operations, Newton paced the deck and, to the furtive amusement of the labouring sailors and the open astonishment of the slaves, he began to sing the words he had penned onto his paper the previous day.

> *"Pore upon your sins no longer,*
> *Well I know their mighty guilt;*
> *But my love than death is stronger,*
> *I my blood have freely spilt.*
> *Tho' your heart has long been harden'd,*
> *Look on me - it soft shall grow;*
> *Past transgressions shall be pardon'd,*
> *And I'll wash you white as snow."*

Ross opened his eyes, roused from sleep by the deep baritone voice from outside his window.

> *"I have seen what you were doing,*

Though you little thought of me;
You were madly bent on ruin,
But I said - it shall not be:"

Ross looked at his watch. It was seven-thirty and the morning light could be seen through the slats in the window shutter.

"You had been for ever wretched,
Had I not expos'd your part;
Now behold my arms outstretched
To receive you to my heart."

Ross sat up in bed, then threw off the bedclothes. He stepped to the window. Cautiously, he lowered the shutter and peered out.

Fog.

The singing continued.

"Well may shame, and joy, and wonder,
All your inward passions move:
I could crush thee with my thunder,
But I speak to thee in love."

Ross could hear the hum of the radar scanners but could see only blurred shapes through the dense fog. He could just make out that there were some figures moving about on the deck below and he thought he heard a metallic clanking noise, but he could see no detail.

"See! Your sins are all forgiv'n,
I have paid the countless sum!
Now my death has opened heav'n,
Thither you shall shortly come."

Then, apart from the radar scanners, all became silent.

Ross laid back on his bunk and closed his eyes. All the memories of the previous night returned. He thought of Yehu and the others still down there in their crude prisons. What on earth could he do?

He dozed. He would overpower Bridson and seize his weapons. Then he would tie him up and go and do the same to the mate, Ian and Bobbie - no, not Bobbie. She would join him in overcoming the engineers and the bo's'n. Once in control of the ship, he and Bobbie would release all the prisoners, who would cheer him and carry him shoulder high up to the bridge to assume his rightful place as captain while they would lock Bridson and his co-conspirators in the containers below. Under Ross's command, they would alter course for New York, where they would be greeted by dozens of fire-fighting tugs spraying their hoses high in the air. The President would greet Ross on the quayside and, with a brass band playing Sousa marches nearby, present him with a medal for bravery before driving through the streets with him in a convertible Cadillac to a glittering tickertape parade.

The breakfast gong brought Ross back to full wakefulness.

Neither Bobbie nor the captain were at breakfast, but the third and fourth engineers were there, tucking into their sausage and bacon as if nothing had happened. At one point they burst out laughing at some joke.

After breakfast, Ross went up to the bridge, where Bridson was staring out into the dense fog while Ian kept watch on the radar screen.

"Reset the guard zones to twelve miles," called the

captain.

"Aye-aye, sir," replied Ian, tapping at a keypad on the radar front panel.

The captain turned to see Ross.

"Ah! I have a message for you to send to WCH," he said.

"Right, sir," said Ross, taking the telegram form Bridson handed to him.

Back in the radio office, Ross tuned up the big transmitter.

Now was his chance. He could not know when or whether he would get another.

WCH responded quickly to his call and he began sending the long, coded message. His operation of the morse key was robot-like. His mind was not on the code groups he was sending, but on how to phrase the next signal - his own - to the distant radio operator.

Thoughts of betraying Bobbie were confused with those of rescuing Yehu. It was a wretched position to be in, but he had to act now.

He completed the message and WCII acknowledged receipt. Ross indicated that he had another message and WCH invited him to go ahead. Ross began with the international urgency signal :-

"XXX. DUKE OF ARGYLL/ELIW. POSITION 13.42N 38.22W BOUND CHARLESTON. SHIP'S HOLD CONTAINS MANY ABDUCTED PERSONS HELD AGAINST THEIR WILL. REQUIRE URGENT BOARDING BY ARMED COASTGUARD TO INVESTIGATE."

"R," acknowledged the WCH operator, "WAIT FOR REPLY."

The long silence which followed left Ross wiping perspiration from his brow. He kept looking over his shoulder to see if the captain or mate would approach. To shut the radio office door would arouse suspicion, since it was always held open on its hook. Ross closed his eyes and hoped that the fog would continue to keep them occupied.

WCH began to transmit again. Ross picked up his pencil and wrote :-

"CAPTAIN DUKE OF ARGYLL/ELIW. ARCTA AALOS R/O PNCEJ CLPQO."

"R," transmitted Ross in a daze.

WCH indicated there was no more to be sent and Ross shut down the transmitter and receiver, and folded up the paper.

A reply to a call for help in code?

The code groups meant nothing to Ross, but the 'R/O' did. It stood for radio officer - Ross himself.

It did not take much working out.

WCH was part of the operation, whatever it was. The absence of records in the official publications had puzzled Ross, but now the implication was clear - it was unlicensed, illegal. Use of the morse-based communication system guaranteed a certain degree of secrecy. Even if by some chance there was a listener tuned to this frequency who could read morse code, they would not think it unusual without checking the validity of the WCH callsign, which they would not normally have reason to do. The code groups had meanings only for those holding the decoding books - Bridson and his fellow conspirators in the U.S. To have used plain language or the normal satellite communication system might have attracted official attention.

There was no way Ross was going to pass the message to the captain - it would obviously expose his knowledge and actions. He thrust the paper deep into the pockets of his white uniform shorts.

"Did you get that message off, Mister Clifford?"

The sharpness and closeness of the captain's voice made Ross jump. Turning, he saw the captain standing in the open doorway.

"Yes, sir." Ross snatched his hand away from his pocket.

"Good."

Bridson went back onto the bridge and Ross relaxed with a blow of air from his lips.

WCH would soon realise there was something wrong, however, if there was no further response. Ross was unable to provide a properly-coded reply and a plain language one would give his game away. He crossed his fingers and hoped some monitoring station had heard his call for help.

If Bridson's masters could not communicate through Ross, they would try the public telephone system via the SATCOM.

Ross removed the fuses from the SATCOM. That way no-one could receive or transmit telephone calls. For good measure, he also removed the fuses from the morse transmitter and receiver. He put all the fuses into his pockets. If someone discovered the gear was inoperative he would have to pretend it was faulty. He could further declare he had not the right spare parts to repair them.

All this would at least keep his cover intact, but it did not solve the problem of how to get help. Sooner or later he would have to transmit a signal to a recognised authority, and that would be very risky.

As he tried to word calls for help in his mind, he began to realise just how unbelievable they would sound when received in the cold light of day in a marine office ashore. He needed more information about the situation before he could convince the authorities that there was an urgent problem. But who could he approach? Ian? Bobbie?

He spent the morning trying to puzzle it out, lying in his cabin, then out pacing the decks. He stood by each ventilator in turn and strained his ears, but could hear nothing unusual. Could he possibly have dreamt it? Was his mind really going, hearing hymn-singing and other voices?

The fog did not lift.

In the middle of the afternoon he returned to the radio office. He replaced the receiver fuse and tuned in to WCH. There was another message for the *Duke*.

Replacing the transmitter fuse, he called up WCH and received the message. It was all in code, with nothing this time to hint at its meaning. None of the code groups were the same as in the previous one.

Just as he was wondering whether it would be safe

to give it to the Old Man, the decision was made for him.

"What are you doing, Clifford?" The captain had entered the radio office behind Ross. His upper lip curled, almost in a snarl.

"Message from WCH, sir. I'll just type it out for you."

"I'll be in my cabin."

Ross typed out the message carefully, keeping a copy for his own files as usual, then took it down to the captain's cabin. He had no choice, and there was no way he could alter the code groups without knowing what anything meant. He felt he might throw up at any minute.

The Old Man was busy at his desk.

Just as Ross entered, one of the deckhands rushed in from the bridge.

"Another vessel within the guard zone, sir," he announced urgently. "On a collision course with us."

"All right, Corkhill. Tell Mister Marshall I'm on my way up."

"Aye-aye, sir."

The captain rose and hurried out after the seaman, calling to Ross as he left.

"Leave it on my desk."

Left alone in the Old Man's cabin, Ross stood for a moment, deep in thought. His heart began to thump. Could some sharp-eared operator have overheard his urgent plea to WCH and informed a naval vessel? There was a slim chance, but Ross was not optimistic. The presence of another ship was much more likely to be mere coincidence.

He placed the telegram on the desk with a sigh. It was all out of his control.

Then he saw out of the corner of his eye the captain's safe, which was wide open. Inside were cash boxes and files. Ross stooped to peer inside.

One file in particular caught his attention. It was labelled 'WCH CODES.'

He heard the blowing of the *Duke*'s whistle. The captain and mate would be kept busy for now, ensuring there was no collision with the other ship in the fog. He saw the captain's photocopier, which was switched on and fully warmed up.

He reached into the safe and pulled out the file. It held about fifty pages, listing each code group and its full meaning.

Unclipping all the sheets, Ross began feeding them into the photocopier one by one.

It was a very slow machine and could only handle one side of one sheet at a time. The machine was not silent and this was going to take an age.

"Oh, God! Don't let this be heard on the bridge," thought Ross. "Keep them busy up there."

CHAPTER ELEVEN

The photocopier rumbled ponderously, the bright green light issuing from gaps in its casing as it trundled out the copies page by agonising page.

Ross had time to read some of it. There were many references to cargo, arrival and departure times - all pretty mundane stuff as far as he could tell.

He could hear the goings-on on the bridge one deck up: the clanging of the engineroom telegraph bell, the blowing of the *Duke*'s whistle, the mate's call "Hard a' port!" Surely they could not contrive to collide with a lone ship in mid-Atlantic, even in fog, with the radar to help them?

If he could hear them, surely they would hear this damned noisy machine. Ross could only hope that they would be too preoccupied to notice.

He tried to think of what he could say if Bridson should suddenly return, but there was nothing. He would be caught red-handed.

At last the final sheet was drawn in and, after the inevitable delay, its copy disgorged.

Ross hurriedly clipped the originals back in their file and replaced them in the safe. Gathering up the copies, he took a quick glance up towards the bridge before scurrying down the stairs and into his cabin.

Removing the bottom drawer from beneath his bunk, he placed the papers on the deck in the gap before replacing the drawer above them. It was not the most original of hiding places but it would have to do for the time being.

Retracing his steps back towards the radio office, he glanced in through the open door of the captain's cabin. Bridson was back in there, working at his desk as he had been before. It had been a close thing. Ross carried on up to the radio office. The mate was on watch alone again and all was quiet on the bridge.

Ross took the file of WCH messages from the radio office and returned to his cabin. Locking the door, he dug out the decoding pages from their hiding place and began to decipher the last but one message, one code group at a time :-

ARCTA: arrest immediately the following...

AALOS: mount twentyfour hour watch on...

R/O was not code, it was radio officer...

CLPQO: will continue to communicate with you by this means where possible.

PNCEJ: if necessary transfer urgent communications only to public telephone using the coded language agreed before departure...

It was much as Ross had guessed. Even so, his neck-hairs were bristling.

His hand shaking slightly, he turned to the latest message - the one the Old Man would probably be deciphering right now. Taking each code group, he carefully wrote down its translation, joining them all together, until he had finished. Then he read the whole message :-

ENSURE ARRIVAL 0200 HOURS AT

159

POSITION FIVE MILES SOUTHWEST OF EDISTO ISLAND. IMMEDIATELY AFTER ARRIVAL ARREST ALL OFFICERS AND CREW EXCEPT MATES, BO'S'N, CHIEF AND SECOND ENGINEERS. ADD ARRESTED PERSONNEL TO CARGO. LAUNCHES WILL BEGIN ARRIVING 0300 HOURS TO REMOVE CARGO. OPERATIONS TO BE COMPLETED BY 0500 HOURS. MAINTAIN VIGILANCE OVER ALL OFFICERS AND CREW. ACKNOWLEDGE RECEIPT ASAP.

Ross's hand shook with apprehension and rage.

Bastards!

Ross folded the paper bearing the translation and put it into his pocket. He quickly replaced the decoding papers in their hiding place, unlocked his cabin door and returned to the radio office to replace the message copies.

Sitting in front of the operator's desk, he did not have to wait long before the captain entered.

"Get this off right away," he said gruffly.

"Right, sir." Ross tried to sound as normal as possible as he took the message form.

As the captain left, Ross looked at the message. It was a single code group of five letters. He did not need to decode that. It would simply be the acknowledgement and he had no qualms about sending it off.

After doing so, he returned to his cabin. He sat with his elbows on his desk, his chin cupped in his two hands.

There was only a week to go before he would be locked up with all those others in the hold, to await God knew what fate. Bobbie, too. Bobbie! He could confide in her now - show her the decoded message to prove she was in the same predicament.

But not Ian. What a good job he had not spoken to Ian who, being one of the mates, was apparently not in the same danger.

The best hope - perhaps their only hope - lay in Ross's radio, of course. It was just a matter of arranging a convenient opportunity. It would have to be meticulously planned, it was no good just blasting off a call for help in the hope he would not be discovered.

Or was he just trying to put it off?

His thoughts were interrupted by the sound of the hymn-singer's voice.

> *"Ensrar'd too long my heart has been*
> *In Folly's hurtful ways;*
> *Oh! may I now, at length, begin*
> *To hear what Wisdom says.."*

Looking out of the window, Ross could see only the swirling fog.

Damn the sod! Would no-one else ever hear it? Or believe that he had heard it?

The tape recorder! In a flash the answer had come to him. Why had he not thought of it before? There was a tape recorder in the radio office, part of the radio room installation. And it was portable. He could easily set it up in his cabin.

He rushed up to the radio office, grabbed and unplugged the recorder and hurried back to his cabin with it.

The singing was continuing as he plugged in the machine, switched it on and held the microphone near the open window.

> *"Approach my soul to Wisdom's gates,*
> *While it is call'd today;*
> *No-one who watches there, and waits,*
> *Shall e'er be turned away."*

The tape wound through the mechanism and the meter needles' movements in time with the singing indicated recording was taking place.

> *"He will not let me seek in vain,*
> *For all who trust his word*
> *Shall everlasting life obtain,*
> *And favour from the Lord."*

"Got you, you bastard!" muttered Ross triumphantly.

> *"Lord, I have hated thee too long,*
> *And dar'd thee to thy face;*
> *I've done my soul exceeding wrong*
> *In slighting all thy grace.*
> *Now I would break my league with death,*
> *And live... "*

The singing was interrupted by another voice.

"Beg pardon, sir."

"Yes? What is it, Mister Hallin?" The singer sounded irritated.

"Washing all completed, sir."

"Very well. Carry on."

"Permission to take them below, sir?"

"Yes, of course, man. Get on with it."

"Aye-aye, sir."

Ross heard nothing more. The recording meter needles hovered around a very low level.

Ross switched to rewind and restarted the machine on playback.

There was nothing on the tape, apart from his own voice shouting "Got you, you bastard!"

So he *was* going mad. Even to seeing the recording meter needles moving. If those voices, and that singing, which had seemed so real to him, were all in his imagination, then he could also have imagined the business in the hold.

And the messages? He pulled the bottom drawer out from under his bunk. The decoding pages were still there, together with his copy of the decoded version of the last message he had received.

Surely he could not be imagining this now? The feel of the paper? The printing on the message forms and photocopies? He re-read his translation to see if there was not some more innocent meaning which he had not recognised before, but there was no doubting it. 'Arrest all officers and crew' could not be misinterpreted, neither could 'Add arrested personnel to cargo.'

He went across to Bobbie's cabin, knocked and opened the door. She was not there. Ross looked at his watch. One o'clock. Could it really be that time? They would all be in the middle of lunch, those not on watch at least.

Ross could not face food. He went down to the wardroom, poured himself a huge gin and tonic and signed the chit for it. Taking it out onto the little balcony, he stared out to sea. The fog was clearing.

He must have been there for over an hour, leaning on the rail and sipping his drink. For long periods his mind was a void, at other times filled with a confusing kaleidoscope of visions of prisoners in containers in the hold, of Yema and Yehu, of messages coded and decoded, of hymn-singing, of Bobbie.

Bobbie! He would have to tell her.

All afternoon he tried to muster the courage to go and speak to her, then dinner came and went and he returned to the wardroom for one more glass of Dutch courage.

He looked at his watch again. She might be back in her cabin by now. He threw his empty glass far out across the Atlantic waters, watching it fall into the swirling foam at the ship's side. The fog had now gone completely and the night sky was clear. He turned and headed for the officers' deck.

"Come in," she called to his knock.

"Bobbie! We must talk. There's something very urgent... "

She was in bed, smiling at him as he entered the room, her beautiful head supported by one hand as her elbow rested on the pillow. Her white nightie was cut low.

"Hi, Ross. I was hoping you'd stop by. Lock the door, honey."

Ross did as he was told.

She pulled the bedclothes aside. It was a very

short nightie.   Her beautiful, creamy-white legs were exposed to the thighs.

The talking could wait.   They had days to spare. Ross quickly stripped off.

She pulled the nightie over her head and tossed it to a far corner of the cabin.   They locked themselves tightly in each others' arms.   He tried to kiss her but she placed a soft forefinger on his lips.

"Why not?" he demanded.

"I'm saving that for the special someone," she explained.

"You're mad."

"Mebbe. Anyway, it's not your lips I'm after."

Ross shivered with pleasure as their bodies cleaved togeather and she hummed with delight.

Afterwards, as he lay with one arm across her nakedness, he felt beneath the pillow with his free hand. There was no gun.

"What was so urgent you wanted to talk to me about, Ross?" She said it without opening her eyes.

"I'm definitely going mad."   Ross knew he should have gone straight into the deadly serious questions, but still he wanted to tread warily at first.

"Mad with passion, huh?"

"No. I mean it. I heard the voices again. Some singing and some talk."

With an upward sweep of her long lashes, Bobbie opened her big blue eyes and gazed at him intently.

"And?"

"It was so real. I couldn't see anything because of

the fog, but it was so real. I got the tape recorder from the radio office and recorded it. I could see it was recording by the meters. Then, when I played it back, there was nothing on the tape."

"Oh."

"So I'm going mad, right?"

"What was the talking about?"

"Oh, something stupid about washing."

"And the singing?"

"A hymn. It's always a bloody hymn."

"What hymn?"

"Search me. I don't know any hymns."

"Always the same hymn?"

"No. Usually they're different. I've never heard any of them before. Except... "

"Except what?"

"Once. While we were at anchor."

"Yes?"

"Amazing Grace. That was one of them. I did recognise that one."

"Amazing Grace. I sure know that one. It's mah Daddy's favourite."

"It's the only one I've heard that I could recognise."

"Written by a seafaring man, too."

"Really?"

"John Newton. Captain of a slave ship in the eighteenth century."

Ross suddenly felt cold.

"*Who* did you say?" he demanded, seizing her

166

shoulders.

"John Newton. What's the matter?"

"That's the name."

"What name?"

"The name that's been mentioned a few times. That's what the other voices call the one who sings the hymns. Oh, my God!"

"Well, that's it then, Ross."

"What d'you mean?"

"It must be deep in your subconscious. You must have read or heard about John Newton at some time and forgotten about it. Yet deep down it's still there, surfacing for some reason when you're under stress."

"I've never read anything about John Newton. I've never heard of him. Did you say a slave ship?"

"That's right. In his later years he regretted taking part in the slave trade and published Amazing Grace and lots of other hymns. Sure, you must have heard the story before and forgotten it - mebbe when you were at school."

Ross drew himself away from her and looked hard into her face.

"That's what this is, isn't it?"

"What?"

"Or am I imagining that too?"

"What are you talking about?"

"A slave ship. Isn't that what the *Duke* is? And we're on the same middle passage as the old slavers."

"Middle passage?"

"The old slave ships' voyages were in three stages. The first brought booze and trinkets to the African coast, the second slaves to the Americas and the third sugar back to England. They called the second stage the middle passage. That's what we're on now. Isn't it?"

She lowered her eyes.

"How much do you know, Ross?"

"About our cargo. In number two hold. That's what I really came to talk about - this hymn-singing nonsense is nothing by comparison. Is it?"

"Oh. You know. I'm glad. I wanted to tell you but I didn't know how much you knew or if you were on their side."

"So! I'm not imagining that, then."

"No. You were the only one left on board who didn't know. Until now. You were bound to find out in time."

"So what's Bridson's game? What is he doing with those people? How are you involved?"

"They intend to use them for medical purposes."

"What medical purposes? Experiments?"

"No. Transplant surgery."

"What?!"

"They're wanted as donors. There's big money in it, Ross. Very sick people can't wait for a donor, but if they have enough bread..... How do you think they can afford to pay us all so much?"

"But if they're to be donors, they'll have to be... "

"Yes."

"I can't believe you could be involved in this, Bobbie."

"I sure didn't know when I signed up, Ross.

Honest to God, I knew as little as you did when you came aboard. I was offered a lot of dough - enough to set me up in my own practice - and I was told I would be looking after illegal immigrants, truly I was. Okay, it was against the law, but it didn't seem so terrible, helping people to start a new life. It wasn't until after we left Liverpool and I saw they were all chained up that it became obvious it was something different. Jack, the mates, chief and second engineers and bo'sun were the only ones who knew beforehand what it was all about. Then soon everybody on board learned what was going on. By then it was too late to back out - nobody would ever believe we weren't all involved. I don't think anybody else cares, they all want the money, but we're all implicated. You too, now. We'll have to see it through. I thought of jumping ship in Sierra Leone, but you saw that place - I wouldn't have been able to trust anybody and I wouldn't have gotten very far. But I'm gonna hightail it out as soon as we get to the U.S., then go straight to the F.B.I. and hope to God I'm in time to save those poor wretches. I haven't been able to tell anyone before, but I can trust you. Can't I?"

"Of course. And all those medical records you're keeping?"

"So that they know exactly which to use as a donor in any given circumstances."

"My God!"

"And to keep them all in good health. That's my personal reason. At least that's positive. I can wipe all the disks before we get to Charleston."

"We can't let it happen, Bobbie. Those poor people!"

"I agree. They don't deserve to die, even if they are low-down scum."

"Why scum?"

"They're all criminals, according to Jack."

"Is that what you think?"

"They only pick up people involved in serious criminal activities. That's the organisation's purpose, so Jack says, to turn evil into good."

"And you believe him?"

"I believe that that's what Jack believes. Some of them have told me they were picked up while mugging other people."

"Not all of them, Bobbie. Some, perhaps. But I **know** one of them personally."

"You **know** one?"

"Yes, she's a perfectly innocent schoolgirl, only fifteen. She went missing on her way home from school in Freetown. I know her family. Her mother's a **saint** who nursed me back to health in the hospital there."

"Are you sure? You've seen her here?"

"Yes. Her name's Yehu. You know her. You saved her from being raped only yesterday."

She caught his arm.

"You know about **that**?"

"I was there."

"There? How... ?"

"I was hiding down there when you came in. I'd just discovered them for myself. Then those two yobs

170

came in and... well, you know the rest. That bloke Brian, too. He's no criminal."

"Ah see."

"And there's something else you don't know. You won't get the chance to carry out your plan when we hit the U.S. They've already thought of that possibility. When we get to our destination, Bridson's had orders to arrest us all and put us with the other prisoners."

"Us?"

"Everyone except the mates, chief and second engineer, and bo's'n."

"How do you know that?"

"I took the message which contained the orders. Look, read it for yourself. I've been handling all the traffic between Bridson and the... organisation, as you call it. They're all in code, of course, but today I managed to take a copy of the Old Man's decoding book while they were all busy on the bridge during the fog. That was the latest message I received."

"The assholes!"

"As you say, there's big money in it. When our usefulness to them is finished, we become more cargo and add to their profits. They won't even need to pay us. They've known that from the start, I'll bet."

"You're right, we'll have to do something, Ross," she urged. "We'll have to answer for ourselves eventually, but it's got to be better than ending up as bits of other people." Ross suppressed a shudder. "You must send out a call for help, Ross."

"I've already tried that. I told the radio station

171

I've been exchanging messages with all about it."

"And?"

"They're part of the organisation too. I should have known. It's an unlisted station. All I succeeded in doing was letting them know they have a traitor on board - and even who he is. I've already stopped them trying to tell Bridson about me once, but I'm sure they'll try again. At least I still have complete control over radiocommunications."

"Call somebody else, then."

"Yes, I'll have to. But it's difficult. Bridson watches me like a hawk whenever I'm in the radio office. Owen tried it, but he must have been caught out."

"How do you know that?"

"Those people down below told me. The last they saw of Owen was when he promised them he would raise the alarm. Didn't you know about that?"

"I had no idea. Owen never spoke to me about it. I wish he had. But I expect he was like us, not knowing who he could trust."

"Well, it won't help anybody if I end up like Owen. So we must be extra careful. What we want is another distraction like the other ship we came across in the fog."

"We're not likely to get many of those."

"We'll have to arrange something." He surveyed Bobbie's lovely face and exquisite figure. "Could you, perhaps... how shall I put this? Could you... ?"

"Seduce Jack?"

"Well, I didn't mean actually to... "

"It would never work."

"You underestimate your allure, my lovely."

"I mean it would never work with Jack. He's not that way inclined. You understand?"

"You mean he's a... ?"

"I don't think so, he has a wife back in the U.K., but normal he ain't. Even if I could distract him some other way, there's still Marshall." She suddenly tensed and looked up at Ross excitedly. "Hey! That's it! After midnight."

"Midnight?"

"Sure. Most nights, after Marshall comes off watch at midnight, they relax in one or other of their cabins for hours, knocking back pink gins, moaning about everything and reminiscing about the old days in their cruise ship company while Ian is on the bridge between midnight and four."

" Now that leaves only Ian. I'm sure I could keep his mind off things for a while. He'd never be unfaithful to his wife, even out here, but I've seen him looking at me sometimes - you know.   I could flirt with him on the bridge for long enough to let you get off a call for help."

Ross looked at his watch.

"It's nine-thirty now."

"Tonight, then. We must be sure the two of them lock themselves away first, then we'll go into action."

"Bobbie... "

"Yes, honey?"

"If anything should go wrong... "

"Yes?"

173

"You've got a gun."

"Sure. Jack gave it to me to protect myself down the hold if necessary. But they've got guns too."

"Even so, keep it with you, just in case. Don't let anyone take it off you. We might need it sometime."

"Okay, honey. Now I'll have to take a shower and tart myself up for Ian."

"Right. How long will that take?"

"About a half-hour, I guess."

"That still leaves us two hours to wait, then."

"Ross, you're not suggesting... ?"

He cupped her breast in his hand.

"Ross, how can you think of that when our lives could be in danger?"

"It might be the last chance we'll ever have."

"Well, Ross, if you put it like that... "

CHAPTER TWELVE

Just before midnight, Ross opened his cabin door and hooked it back, with his curtain over the open doorway.

He heard Ian's door and pulled the curtain slightly aside to spy the second mate going up the stairs to take over the bridge watch from the mate.

A long time seemed to pass before Ross heard the mate coming down, it must have been fifteen minutes. Standing at the foot of the staircase, Ross heard Marshall tap on the captain's door and enter.

"Hello, old fruit," he heard Marshall say before closing the door.

So far, so good.

He went to Bobbie's door and tapped softly. She opened the door and stepped out. She wore the same white uniform as always, but some of the buttons at the top and bottom were undone, allowing discreet glimpses of cleavage and leg to anyone who could lower his eyes from her lovely face. She wore slightly more make-up than normal, particularly around the eyes, and her perfume was more noticeable than usual, but she had not overdone it. She did not need to.

"All clear, honey?" she enquired.

Ross nodded.

"You look terrific," he said.

She smiled, and began to mount the stairs on tiptoe. Ross watched her disappear on her way to the bridge.

After a few moments, he followed, pausing three steps short of the bridge deck, and listened. Ian and Bobbie were out on the bridge wing. Bobbie was talking.

"What a fantastic sight all those stars are. Can you recognise them all?"

"Och, no. Only the main ones," Ian replied.

"Point one out to me."

"Aye. Well, d'ye see yon bright star there?"

"I sure do."

"Well, that's the Pole Star, used by navigators for hundreds of years."

Ross turned and descended to the captain's deck. He listened outside the captain's door for a few seconds - all seemed quiet - then back up to the bridge.

Ian and Bobbie were still out on the bridge wing chatting. Good girl!

Ross crept through the chartroom into the radio office and closed the door quietly behind him.

Refitting the fuse to the SATCOM, he switched it on. The cooling fan was noisy, but not loud enough to be heard on the bridge, he hoped.

Looking up the reference books, he selected the Atlantic Ocean West satellite and the Southbury land earth station. He tapped in the call number of the coastguard. He had to wait only a few seconds before his call was acknowledged. He picked up the telephone and heard the ringing tone.

"Coastguard. How may I help you?"

Ross spoke in a low voice.

"This is the Duke of Argyll."

"Say again, sir?"

"The Duke of Argyll."

"The Dook of where?"

"Argyll."

"A Scottish dook?"

"No. That's the name of this ship."

"Excuse me, sir Can you speak up, please. I can't read you very well."

"No, I can't."

"What's that?"

A terrific bang against the door made Ross leap out of his operator's chair. The captain burst in, his face bright magenta, his lips curling over his teeth and veins standing out fiercely on his temples.

"What the bloody hell d'you think you're doing, Clifford?!"

Instinctively, Ross knocked the SATCOM switch off. Bridson's right hand was in his bulging pocket, no doubt gripping a hand gun.

"Well?!"

"Just calling my girl friend, sir."

"I told you no unauthorised calls of any kind, did I **NOT**?"

"Yes, sir, but I didn't think... "

"You didn't **THINK**?"

Bridson suddenly snatched the fire extinguisher off the bulkhead and swung it above his head. Ross ducked and held a protective arm over his face.

The fire extinguisher came crashing down into the

casing of the SATCOM, shattering it to reveal broken circuit boards inside.

It did not stop there. Ross leaned back in his chair, his eyes popping and his mouth open. Lashing out with the heavy black cylinder, Bridson smashed the tape recorder, the emergency transmitter, the portable lifeboat transmitter and the communal aerial.

"Flaming sparkies!" he raged, "why did we ever have to have you bastards! The last one was just the same!"

Ian appeared in the doorway, which seemed to calm the captain slightly, his anger reducing to a mere bellow.

"I will not have my explicit orders disobeyed!" he shouted. "Is that **CLEAR**?"

"Right, sir," said Ross apprehensively.

"Then do as you're instructed, damn you!"

"Right, sir."

"The only transmissions I permit are those to WCH on that!" His shaking finger pointed at the old main transmitter. "Do you **UNDERSTAND**?"

"Right, sir."

Bridson threw the fire extinguisher to the deck with a mighty clang and stormed out past Ian.

"I want to see you in my cabin immediately, Clifford," he called over his shoulder.

"Right, sir."

Ross looked warily at Ian as he eased himself out of the operator's chair and stepped cautiously past him to the open door.

"I think ye've upset the Old Man a wee bit," Ian whispered, which brought a nervous smile to Ross's features.

Outside, there was no sign of Bobbie. As Ross descended the stairs, he passed Hallin, the bo's'n, heading in the opposite direction.

In Bridson's cabin, the mate sat looking rather sheepish in a chair in the corner, clutching a pink gin, his right eye magnified by the monocle. Bridson was at his desk. Ross stood in front of it.

"Who were you telephoning?" demanded the captain.

"My girlfriend, back in Guildford."

"Did you get through to her?"

"No, sir."

Bridson stared unblinking into Ross's face, his fists clenched on the desk top.

Ian's voice suddenly issued from a small loudspeaker on the bulkhead by the captain's desk.

"What a bloody mess."

"The SATCOM will never work again." It was the bo's'n's voice over the same speaker.

Bridson reached out and flicked a switch on the speaker, which went quiet.

"I want to be informed whenever you enter the radio office on any pretext, Clifford." The captain was almost back to his normal, calm but irritable self.

"Right, sir."

"I shall have a new lock fitted to the radio office door and I shall hold the only key. You must come to me for it when you need to check if WCH has anything for us. How often is that?"

"Four times a day, sir."

"Very well. You must realise, Clifford, tramp shipping is highly competitive these days. Our competitors must know nothing of our movements. You understand, do you not?"

"Yes, sir."

Lying old sod, thought Ross. How much had he heard of Ross's call? Obviously not enough to be certain Ross was not telling the truth.

"Off you go, then, Clifford. Don't try to repair that equipment. The old transmitter and receiver are all you will need."

"Right, sir. Goodnight."

Ross went back to his own cabin. He did not want to go straight to Bobbie, the less anyone knew of their relationship the better.

He turned in to his bunk and mulled over the night's events in his mind.

It had been another near thing. His eyes lifted. Someone up there must be watching over him. Yet he was no nearer a solution to the problem. Without the SATCOM it was now much worse.

Ross was, for the first time in his life, in charge of an almost totally ineffective radio station. Not only could he not send an automatic distress call if the need ever arose, but he could not receive one either, should any ship nearby need emergency help. Not that Bridson or his masters would care.

One thing was on Ross's side, however. Bridson needed a radio officer. He evidently could not operate the old equipment nor read the morse code sufficiently well, and neither could anybody else aboard. So, at least for the moment, he should be safe. If the captain had been responsible for Owen's disappearance, he must have had some anxious moments trying to find a replacement. Ross's presence in Freetown must have seemed more than a stroke of good fortune for him.

Lying in his bunk, Ross listened, half hoping to hear the hymn singer. A nice, soothing hymn might have calmed him. But this time there were no unusual sounds from outside the cabin window. Perhaps the trauma of recent events had brought him back to his senses.

He turned over and over in his bed many times, but finally succumbed to sleep.

. . . .

Captain John Newton was awakened by the first rays of dawn sneaking through the stern window and across to where he lay in his bed. Sitting up, he swung his legs outwards and placed them on the deck. There was still little movement, apart from a strange, indefinable rapid beat-beat-beat which seemed to come from beneath his feet. He had noticed it before and remained mystified. The calm was still over them.

After dressing, he mounted the steps up to the deck, to seek the steward for his morning tea. As he emerged on deck, he caught a glimpse of the vision again through the grey early light. It was only a momentary revelation, but it stopped him, open-mouthed, in the doorway. The fiery furnace seemed to be dormant. Although smoke still issued from its chimney, there was no sign of any fire at the windows. He wondered why it was white, and with a yellow chimney - surely strange colours for the furnace of hell.

Then it was gone.

Newton made the sign of the cross, took a few seconds to compose himself again, then continued forward in his quest for the first refreshment of the day.

By the time he had returned to his room and taken his tea, it was light enough to read.

Sitting at his little table before the window, he gave thanks to God for the ship's safety and the dawn of a new sabbath day. He opened his bible and read the whole of the book of Philemon.

The letter of Saint Paul was a particular favourite, not because it was one of the shortest books of the bible, but because it seemed to have special significance for Newton. It was such a simple, poignant letter, recommending that Philemon should forgive his repentant slave, Onesimus, and take him back into his care.

How Newton wished he could send a similar letter to the plantation owners who would be receiving the Africans who now occupied the rooms below. Yet, even if it could be done, he doubted whether it would save any from the life of wretchedness which would be their inevitable fate - the excessive toil, hunger, and the lash of the cart-whip.

Newton had himself heard a plantation owner

expounding at great length about the extensive calculations he and his fellow landowners had carried out regarding how the slaves should be treated. Their conclusions had been emphatic and unanimous: it was far more economical to drive them hard, with the most meagre of fare, until they dropped, than to treat them kindly, with good provision, until they reached old age.

New manpower was always arriving in ships like the *Duke of Argyle*. If Newton did not do the work God had given him to do, there was an endless number of seafarers willing to do it, and no shortage of wealthy shipowners like Joseph Manesty to provide the wherewithal.

Newton prayed for his slaves, that some kind owner or missionary would teach them of the love of Christ and the way to salvation. At least there was the hope of a better life for them in eternity, if only they could find their Saviour. The last shall be first, praise the Lord!

He often felt he should do more for them aboard his ship, but there was hardly the time to teach them any English, let alone the mysteries of the gospel. All he could hope to do was to show them, through the example of his gentlemen and people aboard, the most humane treatment that the circumstances would permit - certainly a better example than they would ever experience again this side of the grave.

With a sigh, he turned to further prayer - for Mary's safe keeping, for a strong favourable wind, for a new - more welcome - cargo in Antigua, for the service he would be conducting on deck that morning and for the address he would be making to his gentlemen and people. He gave thanks for his own salvation, as he did every day, not merely on Sundays.

His sabbaths at sea were spent as much as possible in quiet contemplation.

He added a few lines to the letter he would be sending off to Mary as soon as he could encounter the master of a homebound vessel. There was not much to relate this time.

The notes he made in his journal were routine, hardly worth the penning.

He sought further inspiration for a new verse to his latest hymn based on Jabez's prayer from the first book of Chronicles, but the right words were not revealed to him.

Turning to read from *The Life and Death of Sir Matthew Hale*, he had hardly begun to absorb himself in the work when a flustered surgeon came knocking at the door.

"Yes, Mister Arthur? What is it?"

"Beg pardon, sir. I regret having to disturb you, sir... "

"I know you would not interrupt me without good reason, Robert. Go on."

"I am led to believe that our drinking water has been poisoned, sir."

"What? Are any of the people sick?"

"No, sir. Not to my knowledge. But man slave number fortythree, who appeared to wish to ingratiate himself to me, demonstrated by signs that some of the trustee slaves had put poison in our casks."

"The devil!" Newton looked at his empty tea mug and placed a hand on his stomach. "Have you examined the casks?"

"Not yet, sir."

"Then do so immediately, Robert."

"Aye-aye, sir."

"Report to me the instant you have done so."

"Aye-aye, sir."

As soon as the surgeon had left him alone, Newton sank to his knees, clasped his hands together and prayed for the wellbeing of anyone who had partaken of any contaminated water.

Returning to his chair at the table, he pressed himself in the stomach. There was no pain, though perhaps a slight feeling of fullness, as if he had already breakfasted. He touched his brow and looked at his fingers. There was a little perspiration, yet the sun was still very low and the morning air quite cool.

He rose to his feet. Was that a slight dizziness he felt at his temple? He opened his locker, removed a small bottle of salts, removed the stopper and sniffed deeply at the open top. If anything, the inrush of strongly-scented air made him more dizzy still. He replaced the stopper and the bottle.

He returned to his book, but before he had read much further he heard footsteps approaching. It was his surgeon, followed by the third mate. They were grinning broadly as they entered the cabin.

"Well, Mister Arthur?" urged the captain. "Did

you find anything?"

"I surely did, sir," beamed the surgeon. From behind his back he produced and held up in front of the captain's eyes a small stone figure dangling on a piece of twine. It appeared to be the image of a little black boy, naked and in a kneeling position.

"And also this." The surgeon produced a second, similar figurine.

"In the water?" asked Newton incredulously.

"Aye, sir. Fetiches. One in each cask."

The surgeon threw back his head and roared with laughter. The third mate chuckled.

The captain managed a cautious smile.

"If it please God," he intoned, "they will make no worse attempts than to charm us to death. But it shows their intentions are not wanting. Check the irons of each slave thoroughly, Mister Hamilton."

"Aye-aye, sir." The third mate's smile had evaporated.

"And make that man-slave - fortythree, was it not? - a trustee. The only trustee. Resecure all the others. We have good cause to show him our gratitude. Had there been real danger - as he supposed - he could have saved our lives."

"Aye, sir."

"Please leave me now. I must prepare for our time of worship together."

As the sun rose into the morning sky, the entire ship's company assembled on the main deck, the mates resplendent in what passed for full dress uniform aboard a

186

merchantman, the hands dressed in their cleanest baggy trousers, striped shirts, spotted neckerchiefs and a ragged assortment of floppy hats, which they removed as their captain arrived before them.

Newton surveyed them with a cautious satisfaction.

He led the prayers and the readings before addressing his captive congregation on the account of his own moment of salvation. He related - not for the first time - of his brush with death aboard the *Greyhound* as it was slowly sinking beneath his feet, of his crying out to God in repentance and of his immediate rescue, both physical and spiritual.

Then, calling upon James Gallagher, his fiddler, he led the men in a rendition of the song he had been trying to teach them for several sabbaths, this time with new added verses.

> *"Amazing grace, how sweet the sound,*
> *That saved a wretch like me.*
> *I once was lost, but now am found,*
> *Was blind but now I see."*

Messrs Marshall, Hamilton and Arthur had learned well and gave forth with fine gusto. Sadly, only half the hands had mastered the full score, whether through stubbornness or lack of wit Newton could not discern.

James Morgan and Robert Cropper seemed to be enjoying a private joke. Gideon Meacham gazed skywards while attempting to move his lips in unison with what he thought the others were singing.

> *"'Twas grace that taught my heart to fear,*

And grace my fears relieved;
How precious did that grace appear
The hour I first believed."

. . . .

Ross opened one eye, then the other. The morning light was streaming in through the slats of his window shutter.

But that was not all.

The massed voices of a full male voice choir also wafted in from the deck outside. He recognised the tune.

"Through many dangers, toils and snares,
I have already come;
'Tis grace has brought me safe thus far,
And grace will lead me home."

Ross raised himself from his pillow, supporting his sleep-confused head in one hand and rubbing his eyes with the other.

"The Lord has promised good to me,
His word my hope secures;
He will my shield and portion be,
As long as life endures."

Pulling himself from his bunk, Ross crossed to his desk, reached out for the strap and released the shutter, which fell down. There was no fog this time. But no people to see either, the deck seemed deserted. Yet the singing continued, as if from directly beneath, just out of his line of vision.

"Yes, when this flesh and heart shall fail,
And mortal life shall cease;

188

I shall possess, within the veil,
A life of joy and peace."

Ross flopped back into a sitting position on the bunk, his bare feet on the deck and his bowed head held in his hands.

"The earth shall soon dissolve like snow,
The sun forbear to shine;
But God, who called me here below,
Will be forever mine."

Then the singing stopped. All was quiet outside, not even the hum of radar scanners could be heard, only the swish of the sea and the distant beat-beat-beat of the engines beneath Ross's feet.

There was a tap at the door, which opened, and Bobbie entered. She was wearing her clean white uniform, all ready for breakfast. He must have looked a mess - unshaven, bleary-eyed, wearing pyjama bottoms but no top.

She closed the door.

"Are you all right, honey?"

He looked up and forced a smile, pushing the recent memory of the singing to the back of his mind.

"Yes. Did you hear about it?"

"I heard Jack going crazy. Then later I heard you come back to your cabin, so I knew things couldn't be too bad." She sat beside him on the bed and they put their arms around each other. "Did he hurt you?"

"No, he stopped short of that, though he had his gun at the ready, the bastard. But the fool wrecked all the radio gear except the old transmitter and receiver which

189

he needs to communicate with his bosses."

"Does that mean you won't be able to call for help?"

"It makes it more difficult. I can retune the set to a frequency someone might be listening on - in the amateur bands perhaps. I should be able to raise somebody given time - and an opportunity."

"Will we be able to cause a diversion again?"

"No chance. Bridson's got the radio office bugged." A sudden thought jerked Ross bolt upright. "Hey! I hope he hasn't got these cabins bugged too!"

"If he had, d'you think we'd still be free?"

"No. You're right. On top of that, though, he's having a new lock fitted on the radio office door and I can only go in there when he allows it, and then only to call the organisation's own radio station."

"So what can we do?"

Ross thought for a moment, then came out with the idea that had been playing at the back of his mind every waking minute since the previous night's escapades. It had seemed a mere pipe dream, but now it looked like being the only possible course of action.

"We'll have to stage an old-fashioned mutiny. Take over the ship."

"What? How?"

"Release those people below. We can't arm them, but perhaps with those numbers we can overpower the mates, chief engineer and bo's'n one by one, if it's organised properly. We've got your gun, and we should get more as each person is captured."

"Wow!" Bobbie breathed, and squeezed Ross tightly. "D'you think we can do that, honey?"

"I don't see any other way. Do you?"

"No. We'll have to work it out. But you look all in. When did you eat last?"

"I can't remember."

"You must eat. Get dressed and cleaned up and come to breakfast."

"Right, doctor."

"Then, when you feel better, we'll plan it."

"Right, doctor."

CHAPTER THIRTEEN

"What do we do then, honey?"

Bobbie reclined on Ross's bunk while he sat in the chair at his desk, holding a pen and staring at a blank sheet of paper. It was now nine in the morning, when clarity of thought should be at its highest.

"I'm not a military strategist," he admitted. "I've never even had any interest in that sort of thing."

"Me neither."

"We'll just have to try our best. How many men are there in those containers?"

"Twentyseven Europeans in one and twentynine Africans in the other. You won't be letting the women out?"

"I don't think so. If anything goes wrong, they'll be safer where they are. And if there are too many people milling around we'll be tripping over each other. Fiftysix men should be more than enough. Now, let's see, we've got to take out the Old Man, the mate, Ian, the chief and second engineers and the bo's'n. Are there any others with guns?"

"Not so far as I know."

"Can any of the Africans speak English?"

"Sure. Several of them."

"Good. We can use them too, then. Can you pick out some English speakers to be leaders and interpreters?"

"I sure can."

"Right. Let's make up five teams of, say, eight

men in a team. That's one team of eight to take out each of our targets. Three teams of Europeans can take on the mates on these upper decks and two teams of Africans can go for Hallin and the engineers. Two more teams can wait in reserve in case anyone else is armed or looks like causing trouble."

"And you say you're no strategist?"

"I've watched the Bond movies, that's all. I just hope to God we don't overlook anything."

"We'll go over it again and again before we hit 'em."

"Right. Will our people recognise their targets and know where to find them?"

"They know the Old Man, the mate and Hallin, they've seen them plenty. Ian and the engineers won't be so well known. They sure won't know the layout of the ship."

"Okay. You and I will have to lead them. That means we can't attack them all simultaneously. We'll have to sneak up on them one by one."

"Gee!" Bobbie fiddled nervously with her buttons.

"We'll have to get the timing right."

"In the middle of the night?"

"Well, Hallin and the chief are on day work, so night time is the best from that point of view."

Ross doodled on the paper as he pondered deeply.

"I think about four-thirty would be best," Ross concluded. "Bridson will be on the bridge, half an hour into his watch. Ian should be in bed and hopefully asleep by that time, having finished his watch at four. Marshall should be right in the middle of his sleep, not due on again until eight. So only Bridson himself will be up and about, and we know he'll be on the bridge. So he must be our first target."

"Sounds good to me, honey."

"Do these people lock their doors when they go to bed?"

Bobbie frowned.

"How should I know?"

"We have to consider the possibility. Do any of the others spend time in someone else's cabin at night, like Bridson and Marshall?"

"Not on a regular basis as far as I know - leastways not among the officers."

"Maybe card playing, or drinking together?"

"I don't think so. Ian likes a drink, but mostly on his own. The rest are sober guys - for seafarers anyways."

"Right. So we assume they will be in their own cabins. But their doors could still be locked. Are there spare keys anywhere?"

"I don't think so. Jack will have a master key to all cabins, I guess, but we won't be able to get our hands on that, even if we could recognise it."

"What about the cabin steward?"

"He might have keys for the officers' cabins, but not for Hallin's. Look, I don't see any reason why any of them should have their doors locked at that hour."

"No. But we don't want any hiccups once things

194

start to roll. We should be prepared to break down doors if necessary."

"Get those poor guys to shoulder-charge doors? You're not serious."

"No, of course not. It looks simple on the movies, but that's stage-managed. It's not so easy when you have to do it for real. I remember one Old Man who I sailed with collapsed in his bathroom with the door locked, and it was a hell of a job to break it down."

"Tools, then? The engineers have got all those."

"I've got some tools in the radio office, but nothing hefty enough. We'd need a sledge hammer or crowbar, or something like that."

"What did Jack smash your radios with?"

Ross looked up at her with a grin.

"Brilliant! Of course! There are fire extinguishers all over the place. You little beauty!"

Bobbie gave a demure smile. Ross was so struck by her loveliness in that instant, that he had to go and sit by her and put his arm around her.

"Now, Ross, we haven't got time for that just now."

"Oh, I'm not so sure. My navigation skills are minimal, so we don't want to go for it until we're within range of some U.S. coast guard ships. That will be about two days yet."

"We can't leave it too long, either. If it goes wrong, we could be too late for a second try."

"If it goes wrong, we won't have the chance of a second try anyway. No, on second thoughts, I think we should make it tomorrow night. Today's Sunday, so that means zero hour will be four-thirty on Tuesday morning."

"We've still got a lot of planning to do. We've got to get the cargo - oh God! I'm using Jack's language now - I mean we've got to get those men in the picture, motivated and ready."

"Right. But that still leaves us some time for ourselves, my love." The imminence of the danger seemed to excite him elsewhere. He placed his hand on her knee. "Who knows when we'll have the chance again?"

"How *can* you, Ross Clifford? You've been watching too many of those Bond movies."

But even as she spoke the words, she was unbuttoning her dress.

"Lock the door, honey," she breathed.

. . . .

At mid-morning, Ross made his first approach to the captain for permission to check whether WCH had a message for them. It was a humiliating experience for someone who had always been free to run the radio station on all his previous ships, where he had always been acknowledged as the expert and trusted to do what was right.

Bridson stood over him as he tuned the receiver and listened out.

As he adjusted the dial, Ross tried to devise a plan in his mind whereby he could still send off a call for help despite the Captain's distrusting presence.

If WCH had a message, Ross could retune the transmitter to one of the international distress frequencies, and send an emergency signal while pretending to be calling WCH for the message. He was pretty sure Bridson could not follow morse, certainly not at the speed Ross would be using.

But WCH had no message, and Ross told the captain so.

Bridson locked up after Ross had switched off and left the room.

Back in his own cabin, Ross cursed his own stupidity. Why had he not *pretended* that WCH had had a message for them?

He would have to try it next time, that afternoon. In the meantime he would devise a simple, innoccuous coded message to 'receive' from WCH.

He pulled out his copies of the codes and scanned down the long line of letter groups and their meanings.

At length his eyes alighted on the perfect message - the single code group: CBKPP. Easy to memorise, it was translated as 'send your noon position daily.' This would give Ross the excuse to use the transmitter every day if the need should arise.

He went off to tell Bobbie about it.

"Shouldn't we wait until we've taken over the ship, honey?" she asked. "If Jack gets wise to it, it could screw up our other plans."

"Yes," Ross frowned, "but on the other hand it would be good to get a message out in case our plan backfires. I'm pretty sure I can do it without Bridson

197

knowing."

"Okay, honey. You know best."

"Tell you what. You get them prepared down below. Get them organised into groups, each with its own leader, and allocate a particular target to each group. Then, if anything goes wrong with my plan you can go ahead alone."

"Oh, honey! Be careful."

She put her arms around him. For a second, Ross thought she was going to kiss him, but just as he prepared to respond, she turned her head away.

At lunch, Ross could only pick at his food, hoping the captain and mate would not notice his nervousness. Apart from the chief, none of the engineers was present. The chief said all engineers and engine-room crew had turned to below - some kind of mechanical fault - and only had time to snatch a sandwich in between working.

In the afternoon, Ross stopped in front of the big map of the Atlantic in the chartroom before approaching the captain, who was on watch out on the bridge wing.

They were about three-quarters of the way across the vast expanse of ocean between Africa and the outer islands of the Caribbean. Time was getting short all right. Ross committed the last plotted position to memory, then went to the captain to ask permission to check WCH for messages.

Grumpily, Bridson unlocked the radio office door and stood behind Ross as he tuned the receiver. With the headphones on, Ross was sure the captain would not overhear any incoming signals even if he could read morse.

"Yes, they do have a message for us, sir," Ross lied, having tuned to an amateur band frequency.

"All right. Call him up and get it, then," growled the captain.

Ross tuned his transmitter to the same amateur band, on a frequency where he felt sure he would be heard by hams on the east coast of the U.S.A.

He began to tap out the message he had in his head. He sent fast, to be doubly sure Bridson could not read it.

'XXX XXX XXX.' That was the international urgency signal. Bridson might have recognised the SOS signal. The captain did not react, so Ross continued. 'CQ DE ELIW DUKE OF ARGYLL REQUIRES IMMEDIATE ASSISTANCE ... '

Suddenly, all the panel lights went out and the meter needles on the transmitter fell back to their zero positions. Ross was tapping a morse key to no effect whatsoever. Both transmitter and receiver were dead.

He swung around to look at Bridson, but the captain stood there impassively. Whatever had happened had not been the captain's doing.

"What's the matter?" snarled Bridson, suddenly noticing Ross's lack of activity.

"Everything's gone dead, sir."

"What?"

"It looks like a power failure," said Ross, feeling considerably more frustration than he could show before the captain.

Bridson turned on the light switch, but the main lights of the room did not come on. Only a solitary lamp glowed dimly - the emergency lighting circuit powered from batteries.

"Did you get the message?" The captain did not sound hopeful.

Ross was quick to lie again.

"Yes, sir. It's just a single code group,"

"Type it on a form and bring it to me on the bridge. I'll have to find out what's happened."

It was even more frustrating for Ross to be left alone in his radio office with his last remaining radio equipment dead.

Keeping one eye on the lights and meters of the transmitter in case it suddenly came back to life, Ross typed his message onto a form, retaining his own carbon copy to follow meticulously his normal procedure.

He was about to step out onto the bridge when the chief engineer came puffing up the stairs and pushed past Ross to confront the captain on the bridge. Ross moved to within earshot.

"Main generator trouble, skipper," announced the chief. "Dropped right off the board. Main engine's OK. We tried to start the auxiliary generator but it won't start."

"When was it last tested?" barked Bridson.

The chief was taken by surprise and paused before answering.

"Only yesterday. It was working fine then, skip."

Ross suspected that he was not the only person lying to the captain today.

"When will it be fixed?" demanded Bridson.

"The auxiliary's seized completely. That'll take days," said the chief. "But hopefully the main gennie will be working again within a few hours."

The chief's prediction proved to be optimistic. Dinner that evening was cold and after nightfall the only lighting was from the emergency batteries, consisting of a few tiny, dim lamps, sparsely scattered throughout the ship.

There was a single tiny light in each cabin, and Ross and Bobbie made love urgently beneath the one in her room.

Afterwards, as they laid back in each others' arms, Bobbie broke the silence as their breathing returned to normal.

"I don't feel right doing this at such a time, Ross."

"You could have fooled me a minute ago," he grinned. "You were well away."

"You know what I mean," she pouted.

"Of course I do, my love. But there's nothing else we can do at the moment. And who knows how many more chances we'll have?"

"Oh, don't talk that way."

"Sorry. But there isn't really anything, is there? The men down below are all primed up, aren't they?"

She nodded.

"There you are, then."

"We'll need to go over it with them again. I'd like you to be there this time too, in case I've forgotten anything."

"Right. Tomorrow morning. Early."

"They don't even know what time of day it is down there unless I tell them."

"I've got a spare watch.   Who's their main spokesman?"

"That guy called Brian."

"Yes, he seems solid enough."

"They're very excited, can't wait to go."

"Good. Is there lighting on down there?"

"Yes. It's not much but it's better than we've got here."

"It might be to our advantage. Without any power, I doubt if any alarm systems they might have would be working. And extra darkness must be good."

"You think they've got alarms?"

"They had the radio office bugged.   But there's probably not much else."

"I hope you're right."

A long silence followed.   Ross had nearly fallen asleep when he felt her hand caressing him.

"You were right to say there's nothing else we can do, honey," she murmured playfully.

Ross put her lovely head in the crook of his arm. He could see her long blonde hair shining and her eyelashes fluttering even in this dim light.

"One day soon, Bobbie Arthur, I'm going to kiss you right on those lips whether you want me to or not."

She gave a shiver.

"Please don't, Ross. I do want to keep something back. You do understand, don't you?"

Her tone was not so emphatic as it had been before on the subject, but Ross did not push the matter further. It would come, he felt sure, if they survived this business. He did not voice his fears on that. It was a time to live for the present, and Ross turned his attention to doing just that.

. . . .

Ross and Bobbie visited the hold early the next morning, while Bridson was still doing his watch on the bridge and most other people were still in their beds.

The prisoners rattled their chains as they moved and there was a lot of whispering.

"Why wait another twentyfour hours?" Brian enquired.

Ross explained that they needed the navigators to bring them reasonably close to the U.S. coast guard ships. He did not mention the fact that there was no radio working. The engineers should have the power back on by the time the ship was theirs. Also, they would be able to use the bridge VHF once they were in control.

Ross spoke to Yehu, to reassure her, and introduced Bobbie to her by name, as a friend rather than as a doctor and an enemy.

They all went through the plan together again. No-one could see any flaws. The hardest part would be guiding the eight-man teams silently to their respective targets.

Ross gave Brian his watch and pronounced him in overall command down below. Then Ross and Bobbie left to show themselves in the officers' accommodation.

After lunch, the captain came to Ross's cabin with a message form.

"Get this off to WCH immediately," he commanded. "They want our noon position each day."

"Is the power back on then, sir?" Ross asked eagerly.

"No. Those incompetent fools in the engine-room haven't been able to fix it yet."

"I can't send that till they do, sir."

"Can't you rig up your batteries so that they will power it?"

"Impossible, sir."

"What about the SATCOM? That works off batteries. Can you fix that?"

"That's not on either, sir," declared Ross with a serves-you-right air.

"Fat lot of good you are, then," declared Bridson before turning on his heel and stamping off up the stairs.

Dinner came and went - another cold meal - which at least gave Bridson, Marshall and Ian something to moan about and occupy their thoughts. The engineers were still busy down below.

Ross and Bobbie spent an hour together before retiring to their own beds for an early night.

Ross could not sleep. He half hoped for some hymn-singing again, but it never happened when he needed soothing. One line kept returning to him, however: 'Through many dangers, toils and snares, I have already come... ' Would he come through this?

Would Bobbie? He tried to push his melancholy to the back of his mind.

He must have fallen asleep eventually, for his watch alarm woke him at four.

He dressed quickly and tiptoed across to Bobbie's cabin.

When she opened the door, he was taken aback by her appearance in a black track suit. It was the first time he had seen her in anything other than her white uniforms. She looked just as good.

"All set?" he whispered.

She nodded.

"Got your gun?"

She patted a trouser pocket.

"Let's go, then."

Down in the hold, there was much chattering and jubilant anticipation as Bobbie unlocked the European men's container and unchained each man, one at a time.

"Can't you quieten them down?" urged Bobbie at Brian.

"We can be heard through the ventilators if we're too noisy," said Ross.

"Shh!" hissed Brian, without much response.

"Quiet!" ordered Bobbie, to some effect.

The European men formed themselves into their three groups.

"Aren't you going to let us out, then?" called a voice from the white women's container.

"Not yet," said Ross. "If anything goes wrong, you can't get hurt here."

"I don't give a sod about getting hurt, let us out of here," persisted the woman.

"Shut up, Sandra," said Brian. "Be patient. And *quiet*. We've got to get these bastards first, and their guns. Then we'll be the masters."

"Roll on," said Sandra.

By now, Bobbie was releasing the African men in the same way. One group of eight formed outside the container but some of the men left inside seemed reluctant to come out.

"Come on, then," urged Brian. "Come out and form your group."

"Those not in groups stay behind, but be ready to join us if you're needed," said Ross.

The last four men emerged from the container, but instead of standing with the rest of their group, they made a dash for the door.

"Walloo-alloo-alloo!" they yelled as they ran. Then, to his horror, Ross saw they were waving machetes above their heads.

"Hey! Come back!" called Ross.

Bobbie took out her gun and pointed it. Two of the Africans stopped, holding their machetes meekly at their sides, but the other two were already running up the stairs, still letting out blood-curdling calls.

"Oh, my God!" wailed Ross. "They'll ruin everything. They don't know where to go."

"Come on, let's join 'em," called one of the men in a white group.

"Let's get the bastards!" yelled another, and two

young Europeans grabbed the machetes from the frozen Africans and ran off. Bobbie pointed the gun at them but did not fire. Soon the doorway was jammed with people scrambling over one another, trying to get out.

"Where did they get those blasted machetes?" called Ross in frustration.

"They had them all along," volunteered an English-speaking African. "They had them strapped to the steel bars so they couldn't be seen."

"We can't get through that lot to stop them," moaned Ross.

"I know another way out," whispered Bobbie to Ross and Brian. "There's a tunnel leading to number one hold. We can get up on deck from there. Follow me."

CHAPTER FOURTEEN

When the chief engineer awoke to the sounds of a pair of howling young black men crashing into his cabin, waving machetes, he assumed he was having a nightmare. The worries about the engine-room generators had given him the excuse to take six double whiskies the night before instead of his customary three, and his brain was still befuddled at such an early hour.

He had opened his eyes but he had made no utterance, nor had his head been lifted from the pillow, before it was severed from the rest of his body by the single falling of a blade.

Suddenly, the main lights came fully on, brightly illuminating the cabin and allowing Baki and Kothong to see the results of their handiwork. Ben and Zitty arrived in the doorway, white-faced, but gripping their machetes determinedly.

"Come on!" commanded Ben, and they rushed to the next cabin.

The second engineer was not in such a deep sleep, having retired only half an hour previously, as soon as he had seen the work on the main generator was virtually complete and needed only some tidying up from the third and fourth and the engine-room hands. He had only just begun to doze off when he heard the commotion next door.

By the time his own door burst open, he was sitting up with his feet on the floor. The cabin lights were

208

switched on. The brightness of the lights and glinting from the blades held high above the heads of Ben and Zitty dazzled him. Zitty closed his eyes.

The second held his forearm across his face for protection but the act was predictably futile. The Pound Lane gang members were not so expert with the weapons as the African farmhands and the process took longer, but the end result was the same.

Jimmy Morgan, the third engineer, mopped the sweat from his brow with a rag before picking up the telephone connecting the engine-room directly with the bridge and pressing the call button. The captain's voice was heard on the other end.

"Main generator back on the board, sir," Morgan reported.

He did not hear the reply the captain made, as he was distracted by a strange noise, even above the clatter of the engines, which sounded like "walloo-alloo-alloo!"

He looked up open-mouthed to see two Africans and two young Europeans in white overalls clattering down the steel steps into the engine-room, waving bloodstained machetes above their heads. He saw Bob Cropper, the fourth engineer, pick up a large adjustable spanner and run to the foot of the steps.

Morgan bellowed into the telephone.

"Help! Sir! We're being attacked here! Some of the prisoners have escaped. They're in here. They've got big knives. Send help. **QUICK!**"

Cropper's makeshift weapon was no match for the machetes. Even though he had to face only the first of the marauders, because of the narrowness of the steps, the African towered above him, an advantage enhanced by the fact that he was standing two steps higher than Cropper.

The fourth managed to give his assailant a crack across the shins with the spanner, but this only served to enrage Kothong all the more. He brought the blade down on Cropper's head. It was as easy as cleaving a palm nut in two.

"For God's sake hurry, sir!" Morgan yelled into the telephone, even though he knew the captain was no longer listening but had, Morgan hoped, gone into immediate action.

But it was not going to be quick enough. The two young whites were chasing the terrified hands into remote corners of the engine-room. Morgan heard their screams as the two grimacing Africans advanced on himself as he stood on the control platform.

Other men were entering the engine-room, standing at the top of the steel steps, just looking. They were not going to be any help. Morgan could see by their white overalls that they were prisoners from the hold as well, a mixture of black and white.

Turning to run from the pair now advancing on him, he leapt onto the steel platform atop the vibrating engine casing. As he had hoped, the Africans baulked at following him up there. But not for long. As soon as they could see Morgan was coming to no harm where he was, they climbed cautiously but resolutely onto the platform themselves.

Before they had a chance to use their weapons, Morgan turned to jump onto another platform lower down, but slipped on the oily surface and crashed down between the engine casing and the platform. His two attackers sprang down with glee and the knives rose and fell alternately, as if in time to the drumming of the engine.

Ross, Bobbie and Brian had slipped along the tunnel into number one hold, which was being used as a food store, then up the steps and into the alleyway where the engineers lived.

Men in white overalls filled the corridor and were shouting at each other. Bobbie nudged Ross's arm and nodded towards a pale-faced teenager who was pointing into the chief engineer's cabin and making a roaring, hysterical noise. Then he vomitted.

Bobbie and Ross looked nervously into the cabin.

"Oh, my God!" said Ross, clapping a hand to his eyes.

Then he heard a rapid stut-tut-tut noise and screams from one or two decks up.

"Automatic weapons!" shouted Brian, gripping Ross's arm. The three ducked into the chief's cabin to escape the melee, keeping well clear of the bloody mess around the bunk.

The stuttering noise was getting nearer and men were pushing back down the alleyway in panic.

"I didn't know they had machine-guns," said Bobbie.

Ross, too dumbstruck to move for the moment,

marvelled at her calmness.

She picked a bunch of keys from a hook over the chief's desk and pressed them into Brian's hand.

"You'd better get back down the hold. Pretend you never left it. It'll be safer for you there. Take these keys and drop them somewhere down there where they'll be found. The chief will get the blame - he won't be caring now anyway - and you must all back up that story. We'll slip away and try again later."

Brian nodded and pushed his way into the crowd.

"Come on, everybody," he called, "back down to our cages. We can't fight those guns."

Ross, recovering from his shocked state, took Bobbie's hand and they joined the mob, but instead of taking the door down into the hold, ran off around the stern and back down the other side, from where they took the outside steps up to the officers' deck and into the safety of Ross's cabin.

They could see nothing from Ross's window, but they could hear the shooting and screaming coming from the decks below.

The firing was getting very close as Brian tried to push the others faster down the steps in front of him, urging them to get back into their prisons, the only place where they might be safe. He trod on men who had been trampled in the crush. Bullets ricocheted off the steel walls nearby.

At last he reached the deck of the hold and began to run towards the container. A terrific blow in the middle of his back felled him instantly, about three feet from the door of the container. He could not breathe and spat out some blood. He threw the keys as hard as he could at the door of the container, watching them land inches from the front of the doorway.

That would do, he told himself.

"Cease fire!" he heard. It was the captain's voice. "Get the rest back inside, bo's'n. We need *some* cargo left."

Cargo? Brian's expression turned swiftly from puzzlement to disgust to unbearable pain.

Then he blacked out and died.

. . . .

"Are all the slaves back in their irons now?" demanded Captain John Newton anxiously.

"Aye, sir," reported the third mate.

"Well done, Mister Hamilton. That was a close shave. Are there any casualties?"

"None, sir. They were all terrified by our firearms."

"Excellent. How did they escape?"

"The trustee slave smuggled a marlinspike into the men's room, sir."

"Did he, indeed?! After we had honoured him? Treacherous dog! Yet he saved us, so he thought, but one day ago."

"Methinks that was a ruse to secure his own freedom and our trust, sir."

"The devil! Such cunning, Mister Hamilton. I must punish him forthwith before his fellows. Have

Mister Hallin bring the thumbscrew down to the men's room. Tell him to seek out this blackguard and await my arrival."

"Aye-aye, sir."

"Good work, Mister Marshall." Newton was now addressing the second mate on his arrival on deck.

"Thankee, sir."

"A terrible business."

"Aye, sir."

"I shall not be sorry to see St. Johns, Mister Marshall."

"No, sir."

"It has been an anxious voyage thus far."

"Aye, sir."

The captain suddenly gripped the second's arm.

"Hark, Mister Marshall," he said in a hushed tone. "Can you hear and feel that beneath our feet?"

The second cocked his head on one side and looked puzzled.

"What, sir?"

"That beat-beat-beat beneath our feet."

"Oh, that, sir. Aye, indeed."

"Then what is it?"

The second was taken aback. He had not expected to be asked for an opinion.

"I... er, know not, sir."

Newton sighed. One trouble with holding the lofty position of ship's master was that people told him what they thought he wanted to hear rather than the truth. The beat-beat-beat was a spiritual phenomenon rather than a physical one, and the second mate was insensitive to such things.

"'Tis the devil's heartbeat, Mister Marshall."

"Sir?"

"Beneath our feet. Coming up through the timbers from the hearts of those heathen in the men's room."

"Oh. Aye, sir."

"Come down there with me now, to witness the punishment."

Newton held a kerchief to his nose as they entered the large room where the men slaves were laid on the deck and on shelves all around, chained to each other, ankle to wrist alternately, with no visible space between them.

Hallin had already singled out the former trustee slave, who sat on the deck, his ankles and wrists chained together and his neck in an iron ring. His eyes bulged almost out of their sockets in terror.

"Apply the thumbscrew then, if you please, Mister Hallin," commanded Newton.

The first two turns of the screw brought no change to the prisoner's expression. The third made him wince and the fourth caused him to cry out. There was a clanking of chains around the room. The next turn produced a scream as the thumb turned purple. Blood began to spurt as Hallin applied further pressure.

"Enough," said Newton.

Hallin gave another savage twist and a cracking sound was heard before the next scream.

"Enough, I said!" thundered Newton. "Damn you,

man! Release that screw!"

Hallin did as he was told, but slowly and with a faint smirk of satisfaction on his face.

"Sorry, sir. I did not hear you the first time," he said, but Newton was not deceived.

"What price do you imagine I shall receive for a slave with a broken thumb, Mister Hallin, compared to one with both hands whole?"

Hallin looked down at the deck and did not reply.

"You will find out, Mister Hallin, when I deduct the difference in price from your pay," declared Newton. "Now, have Mister Arthur see to that man's hand immediately."

"Aye-aye, sir."

"Come Mister Marshall. Let us away."

"The thumbscrew is a dreadful engine, Mister Marshall," commented Newton as he and his second mate emerged on deck. "Would that I did not have to use such a cruel device."

"Aye, sir."

"Especially entrusted to the hands of a man with Satan's hatred in his heart."

"Aye, sir."

"But now we must bury those two who died yesterday. Their departure has been delayed too long."

"Aye-aye, sir."

"Assemble the burial party and all hands who are free."

"Aye-aye, sir."

Oh, to be able to converse with sweet Mary,

sighed Newton, or at least some other Christian equal who could say something other than 'aye-aye'. The only soul aboard who approached this was Robert Arthur, but even conversations with the surgeon were inhibited by the requirements of discipline and protocol.

While preparations were being made, Newton returned to his room and wrote two entries into his journal for the day. The first was brief and understated: 'A rebellion by some men slaves, who had stolen a marlinspike and freed a dozen of their number, was put down without loss or injury, praise God. All slaves were re-secured and the ringleader, number fortythree, put to the thumbscrew.' The second was also brief, and, in part, slightly premature: 'Two women slaves, dead from the flux, buried.'

The burial ceremony itself was a full religious service, culminating with Newton intoning the final words, which he knew by heart from multiple experiences.

"We therefore commit their bodies to the deep. Earth to earth, ashes to ashes, dust to dust..."

The two bodies, sewn into weighted bags, slid from under the flag of St. George, slipped beneath the calm surface of the sea and sank out of sight with barely a ripple.

After completing the service, Newton replaced his three-cornered hat, turned and set off for his cabin without a further word.

It had been a busy day, even for the master of a slave ship.

. . . .

"My God! What are they doing now?"

Bobbie pulled Ross's arms tightly around her waist as they stood at Ross's cabin window with Ross pressing against her from behind.

The captain and bo's'n were giving orders to four sailors who were bundling bodies over the side, each body clad in white overalls stained with red.

"We should show ourselves down there," said Ross. "It'll look suspicious if we hide out of the way."

"Sure. Let's go and act dumb. I'd better go and change quickly first."

By the time they had descended the stairs, Bridson and Hallin had gone inside the accommodation, to where they had seen the mayhem in the engineers' cabins. It was daylight now.

"What's happened?" Bobbie directed the question at Bridson while rubbing imaginary sleep from her eyes with a high degree of acting ability, Ross thought.

"Breakout," he replied. "The stupid bloody chief let the men out. I can't believe he could do such a thing."

Despite the words, it was clear the captain did believe it. At least part of their plan had worked, Ross told himself.

"Are there any injured?" asked Bobbie.

"I don't think so. Not among the ship's company, anyway. They made sure of killing anyone they caught, the bastards! There's not an engineer left alive, they were the nearest."

Two crew members were running along the alleyway laying out fire hoses. One of them turned to the captain.

"All over the side now, sir. Shall we hose down?"

"Carry on," growled the captain wearily. Then he turned to Bobbie and Ross. "Come up to my cabin, you two. We have things to talk about."

Ross did not like the sound of his voice.

"Shouldn't I check the prisoners down below?" asked Bobbie.

"Stuff them!" snapped the captain.

"But we want as many as possible alive when we get there, don't we? It's all money."

Bridson ran a forefinger over his curling upper lip.

"Oh, I suppose so. Go and patch up what you can. Take Hallin with you and make sure you're both carrying. Tell Hallin I want an armed guard on the hold door twentyfour hours a day."

"Sure," nodded Bobbie, then re-entered the accommodation, leaving Bridson and Ross standing together at the ship's side rail. Ross felt only a little less tense. But if Bridson allowed Bobbie to keep her gun, he could not be suspicious of her.

"Do you want me to send a message to WCH about this?" asked Ross hopefully.

"No. Not yet. You know all about our enterprise now, I take it."

"Yes, sir."

"Any qualms about it?" Bridson was eyeing Ross critically.

"No... no, sir. As long as I get paid. They're all criminals, I'm told."

"Correct. Scum of the earth."

"In that case, why not? Turning evil into good, if they can be used to help somebody," Ross commented, hoping he had remembered Bobbie's phrasing correctly.

"Exactly," nodded Bridson, apparently satisfied. "We're performing a service to society, although the authorities, fools as they are, would not see it that way. Hence the cloak-and-dagger stuff."

"Of course."

"But what am I to tell them about this shambles?"

"It was always a possibility."

"They'll say I should have had a guard on them continuously. I just didn't think it would be possible, them being chained up and locked in cages too."

"No."

"But that's what they'll say, the bastards! I know from bitter experience. The Old Man's always the flaming scapegoat. That's what he's paid for."

"Yes, sir."

"I'll have to go away and think about what to tell them."

He turned to leave, then looked back to face Ross.

"Do you know anything about the engines?"

"Not much, sir. What in particular?"

"How to stop the flaming things for a kick-off. And how to put them to slow, and astern, that sort of thing. We'll need to be able to do that before we arrive."

"Sorry. I can't help there, sir."

"The bastards slaughtered all the engineers. All we've got left is a young first-trip greaser."

"He must have seen what the engineers did."

"Perhaps," muttered the captain and shuffled off into the accommodation.

Four sailors carried two bloodstained mattresses to the side rail and heaved them overboard. Two sharks circled around the jetsam.

Ross set off back towards his cabin. The engineers' alleyway was awash with water from the hoses.

He kept his cabin door open on its hook, waiting to see Bobbie return, but he had to wait a long time. The ship was eerily silent, apart from the beat-beat-beat of the engines, which seemed much louder now that everywhere was so still.

When Bobbie did return, carrying her heavy black bag, about noon, she looked weary and her uniform was stained with blood.

Ross pulled her into his cabin and closed the door.

"Well?" he urged.

"Twelve dead," she replied. "Eight injured, but they'll survive."

"God! How are the others taking it?"

"They're mighty scared. But they don't blame us. I managed to whisper to them when Hallin wasn't too close. I told them you'd try to radio for help again. Does anyone suspect us?"

"No. The Old Man doesn't suspect a thing. Amazing! How about Brian? Is he okay?"

Bobbie lowered her eyes.

"He was one of the dead," she mumbled.

"Oh, no!"

Ross put his arm around her shoulders. She dropped her bag and hung onto him as she buried her nose in his neck.

"Are the women all right?" asked Ross.

"Sure. That girl Yehu was asking after her Uncle Ross."

"God! I feel so responsible. Not just for Yehu but all of them."

"They know we're doing our best, honey. They blame those guys with the machetes, but they died too."

"Oh. Right. I don't think I've ever felt responsible for anybody before," said Ross as he clasped Bobbie tightly.

"I guess I'd better go and put Bridson in the picture. If I can face the sonofabitch. Will you get another chance to radio?"

"I think so. The Old Man's going to send a message about it all soon, so I'll do it then."

"Take care, honey."

"Right. I will."

She squeezed his hand and left.

After a few minutes, Ross followed Bobbie up the stairs, past the captain's cabin and on up into the chartroom.

Ian, who was on the bridge, noticed Ross but pretended not to. Perhaps he did not want to talk about the morning's events. Whatever the reason, it suited

Ross, who scrutinised the chart.

They were close enough to assistance now. Some of the outer islands of the Caribbean were only about fifty miles to the west. But time was running short. It would soon be too late.

Ross memorised the latest ship's position on the chart, also the time it was plotted and the course they were steering. It would all be helpful in the message he would transmit when the opportunity arose.

As he descended the stairs again, he paused outside the open door of the captain's cabin and glanced in. Bridson was alone, working at his desk.

Ross tapped on the door. Bridson looked up.

"Should I listen out to see if WCH has a message for us, sir?" asked Ross.

"No. I'm trying to draft one to send to them. It's flaming difficult. I'll call you when it's ready."

"Right, sir."

Ross eyed the modern automatic rifle propped up against the bulkhead behind Bridson.

Now if he could get hold of that... and if he knew how to use it... and if it was loaded with plenty of ammunition... and if...

"I'll be in my cabin, sir," he said, and returned to sit on his bunk again.

The engines were definitely louder now, more of a bang-bang-bang than a beat-beat-beat. It was not just because everything else was quiet.

The pens and clock and empty cup and saucer on Ross's desk were rattling with the vibration. Ross frowned. It was beginning to sound very much like the trouble they had had off the Plantain Islands.

CHAPTER FIFTEEN

"Where's that flaming greaser?"

It was Bridson's voice that Ross heard, together with the pounding of running feet outside his cabin, as the whole ship began to vibrate violently.

Everything was rattling - the window shutter, the furniture, the door. His clock fell to the deck, breaking its glass. Looking out of the window, he saw the structure of the entire ship shimmering before his eyes in rhythm with the awful banging.

The bottom's going to fall out of her, thought Ross, if they don't stop those engines.

How much worse it would seem to Yehu and the others down in the hold, so near the engines and knowing even less than anyone else about what was going on.

Then the banging ceased abruptly. A tall pillar of black smoke issued from the funnel and formed an ominous cloud above the ship which drifted slowly aft. A hush fell over the *Duke*.

. . . .

Captain John Newton was on his knees in his little cabin, his hands clasped tightly together and his eyes closed in prayer. The thumping sensation he felt coming up through the deck, climbing the bones of his spine and entering his brain, had struck him with a terror he had not felt since the *Greyhound* had been sinking beneath his feet. This time it was not for himself - his soul was now safe - but for all the other people under his charge, most of whom did not know their Lord or the joy of salvation. Perhaps if they could have felt the pounding of Satan's heart too they would heed the warning. His prayer was a wordless, soundless cry for help - unformed even in his own mind.

Then, in an instant, it was answered.

He opened his eyes in disbelief as silence and stillness returned abruptly, then admonished himself for such a lack of faith.

"Praise God!" he shouted aloud.

Rising to his feet, he hurried out onto the deck, lifted his eyes and hands towards the heavens and beamed at the blue skies and the little puffy white clouds.

"Praise God!" he repeated softly.

The cessation of the fiendish thumping was not all he found to be thankful for. As he paced the deck, he felt a light but distinct easterly breeze upon his arm. Looking over the side, there was a rippling of small waves.

"Mister Marshall!" he called.

The second mate came running onto the deck.

"Sir?"

"A breeze, Mister Marshall, from the east. Our prayers are answered. See that we take full advantage of it."

"Aye-aye, sir."

The second bellowed for all hands to carry out the master's order.

Soon Newton was grinning broadly as he gazed up into the rigging. The sails flapped, then filled.

The breeze had freshened.   The slight list, the familiar creaking of the timbers and the splash of water from the bow all bore witness to the fact that the *Duke of Argyle* was under way again.

"Beg pardon, sir."

It was the third mate at Newton's elbow.

"Yes, Mister Hamilton?"

"Man slave number fortythree is dead, sir."

"What? The trustee? The one who... ?"

"Aye, sir."

"Dead? From a thumbscrew wound?"

"He has hanged himself, sir."

"What? In those irons? How so?"

"A piece of clothing, sir, cunningly stringing his neck iron to the deckhead above. He must have had some assistance, sir."

"Indeed he must, Mister Hamilton."   Newton's voice adopted a suspicious tone. "But from what quarter, eh?"

"Who knows, sir?"

"God knows, Mister Hamilton, that's who."

The third held his head high, his eyes not leaving those of his captain.

"Aye, sir."

"Prepare the body for burial."

"Aye-aye, sir."

Newton returned to his cabin.   Through the stern window he made note of the swirling wake with satisfaction.   There was now no suggestion of any thumping sensation.   Coincidence?   When God's hand

227

was at work, coincidences tended to abound. However it had been done, the devil's heart had been purged from the ship and they were once more on course for Antigua.

. . . .

Ross looked down over the ship's side rail. The momentum of forward movement had all but been spent and the *Duke of Argyll* was drifting, thankfully in an almost calm sea with only a light easterly breeze. The quietness was so peaceful, after days of perpetual drumming of the engines, and especially the recent excessive noise and vibration, that it was easy not to be concerned about the possible consequences of engine failure.

Only an occasional splash or swish of water could now be heard, and a faint flapping sound, as if someone had hung out some washing to dry somewhere.

Ross went in search of Bobbie but she was not in her cabin. She would be tending the wounded below, he guessed.

Then he heard the clump of heavy footsteps on the stairs. He saw the captain coming up - from the engine-room judging by his oil-streaked face, arms and shirt.

"Are you sure you don't know anything about engines, Clifford?" he asked wearily.

"Hardly anything, sir."

The Old Man grunted.

"The engine casing's red hot," he announced. "We won't be able to get near it before tomorrow. Then nobody knows what the flaming hell to do. The main generator won't work without the engine, so we're back to emergency lighting."

"Perhaps we'll see another ship," Ross suggested optimistically.

"We don't want any other flaming ship poking its nose in."

"Oh, no. Of course not."

"I'll have to tell WCH."

"But we're without power again, sir, without the auxiliary generator or the main engine. I don't suppose the engineers got the auxiliary working again?"

"No. They only just managed to get the main working just before that mayhem and they obviously didn't do that right. You *must* rig up the main transmitter to work off your batteries, blast you!"

"Impossible, sir."

"What about the other gear?"

"Broken, sir. Remember?"

"Well, fix it."

"It's beyond repair, sir."

"A fat lot of good you are, then."

"The VHF works, sir. Off batteries."

"We can't contact WCH on that, can we?"

"No, sir. But other ships. Within twenty miles."

"Out of the question, even if we saw one. You know why." The captain thought for a moment. "Unless... "

"Unless what, sir?"

"If push comes to shove... "

"Yes?"

"We'd have to jettison the cargo first."

Ross bit his tongue hard to suppress a gasp escaping from his lips.

"There's no need for that yet, sir," said Ross as he recovered. "Perhaps I can fix up the SATCOM. Can you telephone them if I do?"

"Yes, if I have to. D'you think you can do it?"

"I'll do my best, sir."

"Go to it, then."

Ross went up to the radio office and scrutinised the shattered circuit boards of the SATCOM with mounting dismay. There was no way he could patch them together again. Components were broken and there were no spares on board. But he made the pretence of trying, brandishing his soldering iron whenever anyone approached. If somebody did manage to restore power while Bridson was not around he might have time to send a quick call for help on the big set.

His evening meal was brought to him and, while the Old Man and the mate were eating in the saloon, Bobbie took the opportunity to look in.

Ross placed his soldering iron in its holder, stood and took her in his arms. They remained silent and motionless, pressed hard against each other, for a full minute. Then they returned to Ross's cabin so they would not be overheard.

Whispering, they brought each other up to date, Bobbie telling of the progress of the wounded and Ross explaining the total absence of radio contact, even with WCH.

"What are we going to do, honey?" Bobbie breathed.

"Whatever it is, we'll have to be quick," replied Ross. "Bridson's already mentioned getting rid of the cargo, as he calls them, if we have to call for help."

"He wouldn't! Would he?"

Ross nodded gravely.

"I'm afraid he would," he said.

"I thought you said we couldn't radio anyway."

"We could on the VHF if we were within twenty miles of someone listening - a ship or a coast station. We might drift near islands within that range."

"Could you send out a call on that before the Old Man hears it?"

"The set's on the bridge. To do that, we'd have to overpower the officer on watch."

"I've still got my gun."

"We couldn't risk it unless we knew for sure someone would pick it up, and the navigators are almost certain to know that before we do."

"It seems hopeless," sighed Bobbie. Then, after a pause: "I'll have to go back down below. Two of the men need keeping a close eye on."

"Right. I'll try and keep up the charade till midnight, then I'll claim the need for sleep. Join me back here when you can."

"Oh, Ross, I don't think I could... "

"No. Neither could I. But at least we can comfort each other and be together if there's any more development."

"Sure. Okay, honey. I'll see you then."

She squeezed his hand and left hurriedly, turning her face away from his as if she did not want him to see... what?... tears?

As he returned to the radio office and his sham work, Ross felt a distinct rolling of the ship. Looking out of the window he could see a choppiness in the sea and the wind was blowing fresher, judging by the bow in his wire aerials and the bending of the whip antennae.

. . . .

John Newton peered over the wooden wall which formed the side of his ship, holding on to his tricorn hat.

"No sign of gulph-weed yet, Mister Marshall."

"No, sir. We be too far out for it, be we not, sir?"

"Not by my reckoning, Samuel. I believe we shall sight land ere noon tomorrow."

"But we been becalmed these ten days past, sir."

"Aye, Samuel. True. Yet by my calculations we have been borne along by a mighty current, faster than if we had been under full sail."

The second mate's face was a portrait of scepticism.

"'Tis the hand of God, Samuel. Do you still not believe?" The captain pointed down at the choppy water. "See the flying fish. I have been watching. In the past hour I have seen a man o' war, boobies and flocks of smaller birds."

"Aye, sir," replied the second with an air of almost insubordinate doubt.

"Post lookouts on the foremast and at the bow all through the night. The moon should give light enough and we shall be able to continue under full sail if we keep a sharp eye open for land."

"Aye-aye, sir."

The second shuffled off to issue what he no doubt considered to be unnecessary orders, but Newton hummed a tune as he returned to his cabin to make notes in his log, to pen a few more lines to Mary and to pray, before retiring to his bed.

. . . .

By midnight, Ross could hardly keep his eyes open. He informed the captain he was retiring for a night's rest unless there was an emergency. It was a statement rather than a request. The Old Man grunted an acknowledgement.

Bobbie was already fast asleep in his bunk when he returned to his cabin. Ross undressed and climbed in beside her. She did not even stir, and Ross was soon sleeping himself.

. . . .

When Newton awoke it was still night. He sat up and saw the reflected moonlight in the rippling wake through the stern window. It was beautiful.

He felt the need to go up on deck to witness the full splendour of this wonder of God's creation, just for a few minutes. He would return to bed later, after his spirits had been lifted.

He dressed and stepped out on deck. He was not disappointed. The wind was very fresh. It had turned but was not unfavourable, and the snow raced through the water. The moon, like a great global lantern, illuminated the entire seascape.

He felt the urge to sing.

"Kings are often waking kept,
Racked with cares on beds of state;
Never king like Jacob slept,
For he lay at heaven's gate;
Lo! He saw a ladder reared,
Reaching to the heavenly throne;
At the top the Lord appeared,
Spake, and claimed him for his own."

Ross opened his eyes wide. He had not been mistaken. It was not a dream. The familiar baritone voice was clear out there on the night air, the strains of the hymn wafting through the window shutter slats along with the rays of moonlight.

"Fear not, Jacob, thou art mine,
And my presence with thee goes;
On thy heart my love shall shine,
From my promise comfort take,
For my help in trouble call;
Never will I thee forsake,
'Til I have accomplished all."

Ross was about to nudge Bobbie awake when the singing ended. He held up his arm, twisting his wrist so the bright moonlight through the shutter slats would illuminate his watch.

Only four-thirty?

But he was awake now and his brain returned to the insuperable problem that was beginning to overwhelm him.

What was he to do?

In his mind he saw the shattered SATCOM, the old transmitter, workable but without power, all the other broken equipment - communal aerial, emergency transmitter, the lifeboat radio...

His mind's eye returned to the old transmitter, then to the new but broken lifeboat radio, then back and forth rapidly between the two. Suddenly, he gave a violent shudder, and Bobbie stirred, as if feeling, even in slumber, the sudden excitement he now felt. But she did not wake up.

All the old original radio equipment had been left aboard. New things had been added, like the SATCOM and the new portable lifeboat radio, but nothing old had been removed. Now, did that mean that the *old* lifeboat radio was still on board? If so, it would be in the motor lifeboat just aft of the bridge on the port side. He had never checked in the lifeboat itself. If it was there, it could be used to send an SOS. It might be their only hope. It would not need mains or batteries, it would be powered by a hand-cranked generator and could be made to send SOS and the ship's call letters as long as the handles were turned. Other ships hearing it could take bearings.

Silently, he got up without disturbing Bobbie, dressed, and took a torch from the desk drawer.

Tiptoeing out of the cabin, closing the door softly behind himself, he crept out of the accommodation and up the outside steps to the lifeboat. Climbing over the rail, he untied the canvas cover of the boat and ducked through the little opening he had made.

Switching on the torch, he peered around the boat. It was very dirty and untidy. He looked under the thwarts, all around the engine casing, then started opening the lockers one by one.

The radar reflector was in one, water and emergency rations in two others, then he opened the fourth to find what he had been looking for - the bright yellow cylinder with 'THIS WILL FLOAT' printed on the side in crude stencil.

As quietly as he could, he pulled it out of the locker and stood it upright in the middle of the boat.

Shaking, he unscrewed the lid and removed the aerial wire and headphones. The aerial should be hoisted up the mast or flown from a kite, but he could do neither. He pushed the end of the wire out through a gap between the canvas cover and the boat's side so that it would hang out over the water. That would be good enough.

He plugged in the two generator handles. He really needed three hands - two for the handles and one to operate the morse key, but he would have to be content for now with sending a basic call with the autokey facility.

He wound up the clockwork mechanism which would automatically key the SOS signal followed by the ship's call letters and two long dashes to make it easy for other stations to take radio bearings. Maybe some ship or coast station or amateur enthusiast would hear it eventually.

As the clockwork began to whirr, he cranked the two handles and watched the output needle flickering out the message. It was working! He took the tuning control between his teeth and turned it to give maximum output.

As the key mechanism wound down, he stopped, rewound it and began again.

He prayed that someone out there would hear it. He put on the headphones to listen for a response.

. . . .

"Wake up!" bellowed Matt Holman playfully as he poked his head around the steel door of the U.S.S. *Hudson Lake*'s radio central.

Larry Walkheimer's face was little more than an inch above the surface of the desktop, as if he was worshipping the radio control console in front of him. His head shot upright and his eyes opened unnaturally wide.

"I wasn't asleep, sir," he protested.

"Okay, I believe you, boy." Holman placed a friendly hand on his junior's shoulder. He glanced at the lights on the console and listened to the hiss from several loudspeakers. "Nothing happening, then?"

"Did you really think there would be?"

"I guess not."

"Why do we need to keep a listening watch when we're in port?"

237

"You know why. The bad guys."

"Drug runners?"

"Mebbe. Illegal immigrants from Cuba too."

"Why come to Antigua anyway?" grumbled Larry. "There's not going to be any action here, is there?"

"No way. We're just showing the flag, that's the official story."

"But why here?"

"It's not a bad listening spot. Just one of many. As soon as one of those boats turns on a transmitter we'll have several bearings and an immediate fix."

Larry changed the subject.

"You been ashore, sir?"

"Just for an hour. There's nothing much in St. Johns for you or me, Larry. Some fourth of July! There are a few clubs, but unless you're a millionaire playboy, you'll get nothing there. You can see for yourself tonight. Me, I'll hibernate till we get to Panama."

Suddenly, morse signals began issuing from one of the loudspeakers. Larry hit a button and noted a figure on a video screen. Matt Holman picked up a pencil and began writing on a pad.

"What is it?" asked Larry as his chief stopped writing.

"An automatic distress call. Did you get the bearing?"

"Zero-eight-one," Larry responded, making an effort to keep the emotion out of his voice. "Is this what we've been waiting for?"

"I doubt it, boy. It's coming from the Atlantic

side, not the Caribbean. And there's only one reason anybody sends a distress call."

"What does the message say, sir?" asked Larry.

Holman showed him the writing on the pad: SOS de ELIW/22, followed by two long dashes for bearings to be taken of the vessel in distress. No other details.

"The twentytwo means it's a lifeboat radio. Very low power." Holman was thinking aloud. "At that strength it's pretty damn close."

"What range d'you think?"

"Under thirty miles. Check the call letters in the book."

Larry plucked a volume from the shelf above the console and thumbed quickly through the pages.

"Duke of Argyll", he read. "Liberian registry. Three thousand, five hundred and thirty tons, general cargo ship, built nineteen-fiftyfour."

"Liberian registry can mean any nationality of ownership or crew," Holman explained. "Liberia is just a flag of convenience - a low-cost way to register any country's ships since only the minimum safety standards are required. Okay. Take the message up to the bridge personally. Stay up there and keep me posted over the intercom. I'll take over here."

As Larry left, Holman tapped an acknowledgment out on a morse key, followed by a broadcast in which he repeated the details to all ships in the area who would be keeping a listening watch.

. . . .

Ross heard a ship reply. Bingo! Thank God! It was a U.S. ship by its call letters, a miracle indeed that any ship would still be listening at this hour.

What he needed now was some assistance, someone to turn the handles while he tapped out details of the *Duke*'s position and the situation on board. He would go and fetch Bobbie to help.

Ross heard a rustling noise behind him and the flap opening. Turning, he was blinded by the light from a powerful torch. He could not see who it was, but the voice which spoke behind it made it clear.

"What's all this then, old boy?"

The torch's beam was turned away from Ross and onto the lifeboat radio.

His vision restored, Ross saw the mate held a hand gun and its barrel was directed at Ross's middle.

"I think I'd better take you to our leader, don't you, old bean?"

Marshall's monocle glinted in the torchlight.

Ross found his voice.

"Look, I was just trying to get assistance. We're drifting helplessly. There are islands not far away. It's dangerous. Don't you think we ought to call for help?"

"Not my decision, old horse. Come along."

CHAPTER SIXTEEN

The intercom from the *Hudson Lake*'s bridge rasped into life. It was the officer on watch.

"Let me know as soon as you have more on this, Mister Holman."

"Yes, SIR." Even as he spoke, new details from another ship came through in morse. He wrote down the information, then turned back to the intercom.

"I have another bearing, sir."

"Go ahead."

"U.S.S. Erie Lake in position 15.36 north, 63.29 west, recorded a bearing of zero-four-nine, sir."

"Thanks. That'll give us an approximate fix. Keep watch and report any developments."

"Yes, sir."

Damn fool, thought Holman. What did he think I was going to do?

On the international distress frequency, the transmission had ceased.

The picture of a ship's lifeboat finally floundering passed across Holman's brain. It could happen to any seafaring man, you just hoped it would never happen to you.

It wasn't stormy out there beyond the harbour entrance, but there was a moderate wind and the seas could seem awesome to a small craft.

It was more likely that the operator was exhausted, he reassured himself. These old lifeboat radios had to be powered by hand generator and it was no easy task to keep turning the handles, even in a calm sea.

He tried calls on the VHF radiotelephone in the faint hope that the lifeboat would be carrying this alternative means of communication.

"DUKE OF ARGYLL, DUKE OF ARGYLL, DUKE OF ARGYLL. THIS IS U.S.S. HUDSON LAKE, IN ST. JOHNS HARBOUR, ANTIGUA. YOUR SOS RECEIVING ATTENTION. SEND MORE DETAILS IF YOU CAN. OVER."

The message, transmitted three times, drew no reply.

Larry's voice came over the intercom from the bridge.

"Distress position is only ten miles from here, sir. We're sending the chopper."

Matt Holman smiled grimly. Larry couldn't conceal his excitement at the prospect of some action, but Matt wondered if the poor devils out there would appreciate that they were contributing to the relief of boredom on board one of Uncle Sam's ships.

"Thanks," he said.

He switched channels on the V.H.F. so that he could hear communications between the bridge and the helicopter. Then he turned to the telex terminal and typed out a request to the international maritime organisation which collated all information on ships' movements for news of the last known whereabouts of the *Duke of Argyll.*

He sat back in the operator's chair. There was

nothing more he could do now except keep a sharp watch. He had been trained to listen out for many things at once, in this case for the V.H.F., three different distress frequencies and the rattle of the printer.

Dawn was just about to break, he noted as he glanced out of the solitary porthole, but it was still too gloomy to make out much apart from lights. He could pick out those marking the harbour entrance.

Then he heard the roar and saw the lights of the helicopter as it lifted off and headed eastwards. They hadn't wasted any time.

There followed a silence which did not seem natural - as if nothing at all had happened since Holman had returned from shore. It was difficult to imagine any life or death drama taking place only ten miles from the placid waters of the harbour.

He suddenly felt anger at the owners of the ship in distress. They had obviously not equipped their vessel with any of the latest equipment. A float-free radiobeacon would have alerted the authorities all on its own. The survivors - if there were still survivors - were very lucky that the U.S. Navy had been listening out, most other stations would be closed at this hour.

. . . .

"Land ahoy!"

The shout roused Newton from a doze. Hurriedly, he dressed again, picked up his hat and eyeglass and ran up on deck and along to the fo'c'sle.

When his eyes had adjusted to the moonlight

243

which was about to surrender to the dawn of a new day, he spotted the dark shape on the larboard bow. As he studied it through the glass, the second and third mates arrived.

"I do believe it is Antigua, gentlemen," he announced with triumph.

"It be great good fortune, sir," said Marshall, still with a hint of disbelief.

"Not good fortune, Mister Marshall. The grace and power of God."

"Aye. O'course, sir."

"The wind has turned again, Mister Marshall. Prepare to tack round the north of the island. If I am right in my judgment, we should make St. Johns before the ebb tide."

"Aye, sir. All hands on deck!" bellowed the second.

. . . .

"I ought to shoot you, you bastard!" Captain Bridson snarled. "Or make you take a jump, like... "

"Like Owen Kavanagh?" ventured Ross with a sudden abandon which he immediately regretted.

Bridson, shaking with rage, brought the muzzle of the gun up and pointed it straight at Ross's head. For a few moments, he glared at Ross, his upper lip curling upwards and quivering.

The clatter of footsteps running down from the bridge preceded Ian's appearance in the doorway.

"Land, sir. On the port bow. I think we're drifting

244

towards it."

"Blast!" exclaimed the captain. "All right, I'll be up shortly."

Ian ran back up the stairs.

"You might be glad I radioed for help," Ross suggested hopefully.

"Shut up, you! Sam, give him one of your potions, and send for Hallin."

"Certainly, old fruit," said the mate.

Bridson continued to point the gun at Ross while the mate telephoned the bo's'n, then mixed a cocktail of spirits and pills taken from the Old Man's cupboard. He handed it to Ross.

"Drink," ordered the captain.

Ross hesitated.

"It won't kill you, more's the pity," growled Bridson. "It'll keep you quiet till I've decided whether to shoot you or not. Now drink, blast you!"

Ross did as he was told, giving a choking cough as he attempted to swallow.

"Don't spit any out!" threatened the captain, bringing the muzzle of the gun up to Ross's chin.

"Now count aloud up to five," he ordered as Ross finished draining the glass.

Ross obeyed as the bo's'n came running up the stairs, gun in hand.

"Lock this bastard in his cabin and mount guard on the door," commanded Bridson, handing Hallin his master key.

"Aye-aye, sir," replied the bo's'n. Turning his gun

on Ross, he motioned to him to descend the stairs.

Shoving Ross into his cabin, Hallin slammed the door and Ross heard the key turn in the lock. It was a futile thing to do, since Ross could easily open it by turning the knob on the inside, but no-one on board seemed to be thinking straight. It would not do any good with an armed man outside the door anyway.

Ross put a hand to his head. He sat down heavily in the chair at his desk.

"What is it, honey? What's wrong now?"

Bobbie! Ross had forgotten she was there in his bed. She must have been covered up. Hallin had not noticed her presence.

"I might have blown it, Bobbie." Ross slurred the words. "But I got a dishtresh message out. And it was picked up."

"Great! How?"

"I found an old lifeboat radio in the port boat."

"Wonderful!"

"But the monocled maniac caught me in the act and took me to Bridson. He had a gun. They made me drink some stuff... it's going to knock me out, I think."

"Quick! Over to the sink. Stick your fingers down your throat."

Ross did as he was told, retched and brought up some fluid.

"Walk up and down," Bobbie urged.

As he tried to do so, Ross seemed to float across the cabin, as if he had springs on his shoes.

The ship lurched, and he grabbed hold of the desk

for support.

"We're going to run aground," he announced, as if it was the most natural course of events.

"Aground?"

"There's land."

Bobbie lowered the window shutter and peered out. Dawn had broken.

. . . .

During the next ten minutes, the light of dawn quickly flared. The harbour entrance and the yachts moored inside became clearly visible to Matt Holman and the navigation lights at the entrance were reduced to mere twinkles with no blackness to provide contrast.

Suddenly the printer chattered into life. Holman stepped across to read the message.

'RE DUKE OF ARGYLL/ELIW. DEPARTED CHARLESTON, SOUTH CAROLINA, 4 MAY, DESTINATION LIVERPOOL, ENGLAND. LEFT THERE 2 JUNE, DESTINATION CAPE TOWN, SOUTH AFRICA.'

Holman frowned, it was now the fifth of July. The printer continued. **'FOLLOWING SIGNAL RECEIVED BY RADIO AMATEURS FROM ELIW, 1 JULY, 2134 GMT: URGENT DUKE OF ARGYLL REQUIRES IMMEDIATE ASSISTANCE ... (TRANSMISSION CEASED). NO BEARING RECORDED. EFFORTS TO CONTACT VESSEL SINCE HAVE BEEN UNSUCCESSFUL.'**

Holman passed the information on to the bridge.

His face was grim.   More than three days in trouble. Those guys would be in bad shape.

Suddenly, the voice of the chopper pilot broke through the silence on the V.H.F.

"Helicopter to Hudson Lake. I have a sighting."

"The lifeboat?" prompted the voice of the officer on the bridge.

"Negative. The ship herself. Listing to port but not in immediate danger. I'm going in to take a closer look."

"Keep an eye open for lifeboats as well, Kolinsky."

"SIR!"

After a pause, the pilot's voice returned.

"Lifeboats all in position on board mother vessel," he reported. "Name checked - it's the Duke of Argyll all right, registered Monrovia. No sign of fire or damage."

Another pause.

"There's something strange here, sir," the pilot resumed. "The ship seems to be under way, listing to port, heading southwest."

"What's strange, Kolinsky?"

"The screw isn't turning, sir. It came out of the water in the swell and it was stationary. Yet she's making about ten knots.   Heading straight for the rocks at Beggar's Point."

"Must be the tide. I'll order the harbour tug and lifeboat to come out."

"They'll never be here on time, sir. At the rate she's going, she'll be aground in ten minutes."

"I'll do it anyway." Pause. "Any sign of life on board?"

"I'll have to go down closer, sir."

"Don't endanger your aircraft."

"No, sir!" Then, suddenly the pilot's voice became a shout. "Wow! What the hell...?"

"What's the matter, Kolinsky?"

"She's swinging round."

"What d'you mean?"

"She's altered course. Swung right around. Took us by surprise. She's now heading northwest, away from the rocks. She's listing the other way now - to starboard."

"Cargo shifted maybe. But she must be under power to make a manouevre like that."

. . . .

Bobbie opened the cabin window, stuck her head out and looked in all directions.

"I don't see any land, honey."

"Port bow."

"I can't see that from here."

"Ne'er mind. Trus' me. Hey! Look out there!"

Ross moved to the window beside her.

The two looked out towards the stern, Ross beaming broadly, Bobbie with a puzzled frown.

"What is it, honey?"

"Sails."

"What?"

"Masts and sails. Lots of 'em. We've sprouted masts and sails."

"I don't see anything, honey."

"Yes, you musht. Look... little men running up and down the ropes, with their baggy trousers... striped shirts... woolly nightcaps... wheeeeee... "

"Sit down, honey."

"No. Look. Thish is good. See that bloke with the three-cornered hat and puffy trousers? Listen. He's singing. It's the hymn-singer, Bobbie! It's Newton!"

"Ross... "

"Come on. Let's join in."

Ross began to sing in a croaky, slurred voice.

"... *I once was lost, but now am found,*
Was blind, but now I see.
'Twas grace that taught my heart to fear,
And grace my fears relieved... "

"Ross, stop it, please honey. Hallin will hear."

"Sod Hallin. Look! They're turning the sails."

The ship gave another lurch. Both Ross and Bobbie had to take a corrective stance as the list changed from starboard to port.

"Come on. Give him a wave," grinned Ross, leaning out of the window and flourishing his hand.

"Ross! Look! A helicopter!" Bobbie exclaimed.

"Eh? No. It's just the sails flapping."

"No, honey. Up there. Can't you hear it?"

. . . .

"Anything new, Kolinsky?" demanded the voice from the bridge.

"I'm moving down again for a closer look. At

least she won't run aground now. I agree she's under way somehow, but the screw's definitely not turning..." The pilot broke off and his excitement suddenly increased. "There's somebody on the foredeck, sir. I'm almost alongside her now. Hell, sir! There's a guy on deck in costume!"

"Don't fool around, Kolinsky. This is serious."

"I'm not kidding, sir. There's a guy wearing a three-cornered hat, long coat and boots. Standing on the fo'c'sle head."

"You on some kind of dope, Kolinsky?"

"It's true, sir. Jeez, they must have had some party aboard that ship last night. I don't think he's even seen me - he's just staring straight ahead."

"Anybody else there?"

"Negative. Not a sign. Oh, correction."

"Well?"

"I don't know, sir. I thought I saw a movement at a window, but I'm not... Whey!"

"What now?"

Silence.

"Kolinsky?"

Silence.

"Kolinsky! Something wrong?"

Silence.

"Kolinsky! Report immediately."

The pilot's voice resumed.

"Sorry, sir. I had to take sudden evasive action. The ship swung round again. Her mast nearly touched me."

"Okay. Stay clear but keep reporting. Where's she heading now?"

"Towards Boon Point. She's on the same course as when we first sighted her - southwest. She's listing to port again now."

"**Another** cargo shift?"

"If it is, she's carrying a mighty unstable cargo, sir. It looks more... well, deliberate."

"Why should she deliberately head for the rocks, Kolinsky?"

"Your guess is as good as mine, sir."

"Okay. Stay close, but not too close."

"Yes, sir."

"Any more people sightings?"

"Negative, sir. The weird guy's disappeared from the foredeck. No sign of the tug yet."

"They're still trying to get a crew together. We've sent some men over ourselves."

"It'll be too late, sir. She'll be on the rocks in a few minutes."

"The harbour lifeboat's been launched. Just leaving now."

Holman looked through the porthole. The tough little craft pitched into the swell as it left the harbour mouth.

"Hey!" yelled the pilot, his shout distorting the radio signal. "She's swung again. Northwest course. List to starboard." Pause. "Hey, sir, I hate to suggest this, but do you know what I think she's doing?"

"Go on, Kolinsky."

"She's tacking, sir."

"Tacking?!"

"Yes, sir."

"Don't be ridiculous, Kolinsky. If you're bullshitting me I'll have you put on a charge."

"No bull, sir. That's the way it looks from here. She's tacking round the coast."

"She must have rigged a sail, then."

"Negative. No sign of a sail, sir."

"Goddam it, this doesn't make sense. You'd better be able to explain when we do find out what's been..."

"Wait, sir. I see the funny guy again. He's on the fo'c'sle, leaning right over the bow."

The voice of the officer on the bridge assumed a sarcastic tone.

"Impersonating a figurehead or throwing up?"

The pilot ignored the remark.

"Altering course again, sir. Heading s o u t h w e s t, list to port again. She should clear the island now if she carries on this way."

Silence.

"Oh, some people appearing on deck, sir."

"Go on, Kolinsky."

"They're jettisoning cargo, I think."

"What cargo?"

"Nothing big, sir. I can't quite make it out, but it looks like a lot of metal junk."

. . . .

"You must see the helicopter, honey. Look!"

253

"It's only the sails," Ross repeated, and began to sing again.

"Through many dangers, toils and snares
I have already come;
'Tis grace has brought me safe thus far,
And grace will lead me home.

Look out!"

Ross ducked.

"What is it now, honey?"

"Didn't you see? He took his hat off and threw it straight at me. Did it come in here?"

"No, honey. Sit down, please."

"Not now. Look at him strutting up and down, singing at the top of his voice. See the sailors, dozens of 'em."

"It's a helicopter, baby." She put her arms around him. "We'll soon be safe."

"Ha-ha!" Ross leaned out of the window and waved again before singing once more.

"The earth shall soon dissolve like snow,
The sun forbear to shine;
But God, who called me here below,
Will be forever mine.

They're going! No, don't go!"

"What's going, honey?"

"The bloke Newton, and all the men, and the sails and the masts. They just dissolved. Like snow, as the song said."

Ross sat down in the chair, the beaming smile replaced by a puzzled look.

"Are you feeling better now, honey?"

"I'm okay." Ross suddenly jumped up again and looked out of the window. "Hey! There's a helicopter!"

"Yes, honey. You see it now?"

"Of course. They must have acted on my call. But where's Newton gone?"

"It's the U.S. Navy."

"Right. They'll send a tug now, I expect."

"Sure. Come here, honey."

She took Ross's head and clasped it to her bosom. For the first time, Ross noticed she was still wearing her skimpy nightie. He wrapped his arms around her and held her tightly.

"Didn't you hear him singing?" he asked, almost pleading.

"I heard you singing."

"I was following him. I don't know all the words of Amazing Grace, so that proves he was there. Doesn't it?"

"They weren't the right words, honey."

"What d'you mean, not the right words?"

"That stuff about the earth dissolving like snow. It's not in the song."

"It must be."

"No, honey. I know it all off by heart, mah Daddy saw to that. The last verse goes: When we've been there ten thousand years, bright shining as the sun; we've no less days to sing God's praise, than when we first begun."

"He didn't sing that."

"No, honey."

255

"He wouldn't. It's ungrammatical."

"What d'you mean?"

"'No less days.' It's not right. It should be 'no fewer days.'"

"If you say so, honey."

"Oh, sorry. What are we doing? Our first tiff - about the words of a hymn, of all things."

"That's okay. You feeling better now, Ross?"

"I feel a bit sick and dizzy, but not too bad. Is the helicopter still around?"

They turned back to the window.

"Yes. See, hovering over there." Bobbie pointed.

"There's the land."

"Sure."

"We seem to be under way, too. I wonder if we're being towed. I don't like this list. It seems to change every so often."

"Hey! Look!" Bobbie interrupted. "It's Bridson and the mate."

"What are they doing?" asked Ross, trying to get a better view of the starboard side of the main deck.

They watched in silence as the two men strolled across the deck, hand in hand, to the starboard rail. They both climbed up and stood precariously on the wooden top rail.

The captain pulled a pistol from his pocket and held it to the mate's head. The mate's body gave a jerk, a spurt issued from his head and his monocle flew up in the air, glinting in the rays of the morning sun.

They heard the crack.

Bridson gave the mate's body a push to send it down over the side. Then he put the gun to his own head and allowed himself to tip, head forward, out of sight over the side.

They heard the second crack.

Neither Ross nor Bobbie could bring themselves to comment directly on what they had seen.

"I can't see any other ships," said Bobbie absently.

. . . .

The helicopter pilot continued his reports as he followed the ship's wayward progress, until it became clear they would soon appear within sight of the *Hudson Lake* herself.

Holman opened a drawer and pulled out a pair of binoculars. Stepping close to the porthole, he lifted them to his eyes, directing his gaze towards the harbour entrance and adjusting the focus.

For a long time, he saw nothing new and his arms began to ache. He was just about to lower the binoculars when he saw the bow of a ship appear beyond the northern limit of the entrance.

The chopper pilot's voice broke in again.

"She's altering again, sir. To port. Now heading east, straight for the harbour entrance."

Holman saw the manouevre himself. The ship was turning bow on to his line of sight.

"Hell sir!" the pilot went on, as if to confirm Holman's thoughts, "if she enters harbour out of control she'll cause havoc. She could even ram the Hudson

Lake."

"We're on alert, Kolinsky. I see her now. We can manouevre if necessary. I can't say the same for the moored yachts. I hope there's nobody on board any of them. I'll try to warn them."

. . . .

Suddenly, the cabin door opened, and Hallin came in, his gun pointing at the deck.

"Oh!" He started at the sight of Bobbie and his eyes roved over her scantily clad figure. He looked at Ross as if struggling to come to terms with the situation.

"The Old Man and the mate have gone," he said.

"We know," said Bobbie.

"Left us to carry the can," Hallin went on.

"Us?" queried Ross.

"That's right. We're drifting into a harbour entrance. Quite a town. And the Yankee Navy's there. You can come out. Go and see for yourselves."

Before they could do so, Ian Hamilton came along the alleyway towards them. He also carried a gun.

"We haven't got much time left," he said. "I must fill you in on what's happened."

"We saw Bridson and the mate go," said Ross.

"Aye. That makes things a mite easier for the rest o' us. I've done a deal with the prisoners."

"A deal?" queried Ross.

"Aye. They've agreed to say they were voluntary passengers, trying to enter the U.S. illegally."

"How on earth did you get them to agree to that?"

Ross pressed.

"That way they'll no' be blamed for the engineers' deaths."

"But only a handful of them were involved in that, and it could be justified in the circumstances."

"Aye. They took some persuading, especially the women. But all they really want is to be sent home as quickly as possible and I pointed out that a lengthy inquiry could delay that for months or even years if they were suspected of anything more serious. It'll take the pressure off the rest o' us - we might face charges, but with the Old Man and the mate gone, we're only small fry. I ken they'll just pack us off home as well."

"Four engineers too," Ross reminded him. "How are we going to explain that?

"Och, we'll just have to say they jumped overboard with the Old Man and the mate."

"They'll never believe that."

"Mebbe not. But they won't be able to prove otherwise, will they?"

"What about the chains and handcuffs and all that?" Bobbie persisted.

"All over the wall," Ian explained. "All ship's papers shredded and all other evidence destroyed."

"And the containers themselves?"

"We've taken all the locks off, pegged back the doors and put some mattresses and blankets inside to make them look more like temporary accommodation. They look quite cosy now."

"My computer?"

"Aye. All taken care on."

"I hope you've thought of everything."

"I canna think o' anything else."

"What about those guns?"

"Aye. They can go now."

Ian and Hallin stepped out of the alleyway onto the deck and threw their weapons far out over the ship's side.

. . . .

The bow of the snow dipped ever more gently into the calming waters as the *Duke of Argyle* entered harbour. Captain John Newton stood triumphantly on the fo'c'sle head.

"By the grace of God, St. Johns!" he called out, to no-one in particular. Then, to the third mate who stood nearby, "Where did my tricorn go, Mister Hamilton?"

"There's no sign of it, sir. The men have searched the decks. It must have gone overboard."

"Dear me! I must desist from such foolish behaviour. I now have only one hat remaining."

"Aye, sir."

"But see what a pleasant sight the land is. Open up all the hatches and prepare to drop anchor."

"Aye-aye, sir."

. . . .

Ross put his arm around Bobbie's shoulders as they stood with Hallin at the side rail of the *Duke of Argyll*. Bobbie had taken time to dress up in her white

260

uniform, but Ross was still unkempt and unshaven, the dirt from the lifeboat still on his shirt and shorts.

They watched the eerie sight of their ship drifting helplessly, yet with such uncanny good fortune, into the entrance of a sheltered harbour. A lifeboat from shore moved around the *Duke* and the helicopter hovered overhead. The three waved at both.

"Where are we?" Bobbie asked.

"I think it's St. Johns, Antigua," replied Hallin.

"Antigua!" gasped Ross.

Bobbie failed to notice Ross's brief astonished expression.

"What's going to happen now?"

"There's a U.S. Navy ship over there," Hallin pointed. "That's where the chopper's come from. We're going to have a lot of explaining to do. In the meantime, I'd better go and drop the pick before we hit something."

The bo's'n ambled off forward.

"He's right," said Bobbie. "D'you think they'll believe us?"

"From what Ian said, it looks like they might, if none of the prisoners grasses on us. Even if they do, Yehu will speak up for us."

"I hope you're right, honey."

They watched the white overalled ex-prisoners emerging onto the deck.

. . . .

Holman heard the *Hudson Lake*'s siren sounding shrilly. At the same time, he saw what he took to be the

Duke of Argyll getting much closer - heading through the harbour entrance and towards the *Hudson Lake*. He also saw the chopper hovering nearby.

Kolinsky's voice resumed over the intercom.

"She's slowing, sir."

"Thank God for that."

"Hey, sir! Three people have just come out on deck. Can you see them? Two men and a woman. They've seen me. They're waving. I'm not invisible after all."

"Estimated speed?"

"Dead slow now. Two knots maybe. More people coming out on deck. Lots of them in white overalls. She's pretty crowded for a small ship."

"Okay. Return to Hudson Lake, Kolinsky."

"SIR!"

Holman watched as the ship reached the middle of the harbour. Figures were crossing her decks. Suddenly her anchor fell into the placid water with a clanking roar loud enough for Holman to hear through the closed porthole, sending up a great cloud of rust.

She swung around on the anchor and he examined her side.

The name *Duke of Argyll* was plain enough on her bow. She was small, little more than a coaster - green hull, streaked with rust, rounded white upperworks and a plain yellow funnel. She was elderly - an early 'fifties coastal cargo vessel, as the book had said. There was nothing visibly wrong with her.

The helicopter had returned to its mother ship and

Holman saw the lifeboat heading back into the harbour. Soon a launch from the *Hudson Lake* was making for the new arrival.

. . . .

Yehu suddenly appeared on deck, ran up to Ross and flung her arms around his neck.

"Thank you, Uncle Ross. You saved us, didn't you?"

"I did manage to send a distress message," he said modestly, "but I think someone up there was looking after us too."

She gave Ross a big kiss on the lips. Ross noticed Bobbie was watching with a frown.

"Now you run along and join the others."

"Can't I stay with you, Uncle Ross?"

"No. The police will want to question us, I expect. You go with the others, you'll soon be home. Give my love to your mother."

"Won't I see you again?"

"We'll have to see."

"All right, Uncle Ross. Goodbye, then."

"Goodbye, little one," said Ross, wiping his eye as Yehu walked reluctantly away.

"Now comes the time of reckoning," Bobbie commented with a slight shiver.

"Don't worry. It'll work out just as Ian said if we all keep our heads."

"I hope you're right, honey."

"What makes me so mad is the thought that those

faceless bastards at WCH will get away scot free. Free to try it again some day."

"Mah daddy would have had the answer to that one, honey."

"Oh?"

"Whenever he encountered injustice, he would just say: 'Vengeance is mine, saith the Lord. I will repay.' A bible quote. Then he could walk away and forget all about it."

"Hmm. I've heard that before somewhere. You love your daddy, don't you, Bobbie."

"Sure, honey," she smiled.

. . . .

Holman saw another figure appear on the main deck of the freighter and heave a rope ladder down the side. Five men in smart, tropical U.S. Navy uniforms climbed aboard her, while three others remained in the launch.

A new voice came over on the V.H.F.

"Boarding party to Hudson Lake. Now on board. There are dozens of people here, some European, some African. We're going into the accommodation to investigate further."

"Understood," came the reply from the bridge.

The hand-held V.H.F. set would be unable to transmit effectively from within the steel structure of the *Duke of Argyll*'s accommodation, so Holman sat back in the operator's chair and prepared for a long wait. He spent some time writing up details in the radio log.

Returning to the porthole after he had finished, he once more trained his binoculars on to the *Duke of Argyll*.

The boarding party reappeared on deck. Dozens more people, all wearing white overalls, began pouring out of the accommodation and onto the main deck. The V.H.F. came to life again.

"Continuing to search, sir."

. . . .

Ross watched as Yehu and the other ex-detainees made their way to the gangway. Then he took Bobbie in his arms.

"What are you going to do when this is over?" he asked.

"Go home to mah Daddy, honey," she said wistfully. "He'll be glad to have me back."

"I'd like to meet your Daddy too," said Ross.

"You would?"

"Right."

"Why?"

"You said he's a preacher."

"Sure. So?"

"I'd like him to tell me all about John Newton. Er, and God."

"He'd sure do that, honey, but he wouldn't stop there."

"What d'you mean?"

"He'd go on to tell you all about Jesus and how he died on the cross to save you once you have repented of your sins and asked his forgiveness - God's that is. Would you be ready for that?"

"That's OK. It's probably overdue in my case. All I've heard about that stuff is what blokes have said in the pub. I remember seeing a sign outside a church once - the wages of sin is death, it said. It made me feel a bit uneasy."

"That's only the first part, honey. It goes on - but the gift of God is eternal life in Christ Jesus."

"I should have tried to find out more before, I suppose."

"You could always just read the Bible."

"Don't know whether I'd understand it."

"'Course you would, honey."

"You must know all about it."

"I was brought up with it, honey. But when that happens, young folk often rebel, as I have. I guess I wanted to have my share of sinning, there'd be plenty of time to confess it all later. But I could end up like those poor engineer guys before I had a chance."

"Hmm. Can your Daddy marry people?"

"Of course. He has the authority to... Hey, did you have anyone in mind?"

"I've been aching to kiss you properly ever since I first set eyes on you, Bobbie. If the only way I'm going to be able to do that is through marriage, then that's what I'll have to do."

"What a dumb proposal!" Bobbie lifted his chin with her forefinger. "You don't have to do that, honey," she breathed, and planted her full red lips on Ross's mouth.

"Now, d'you want to go back on that rash statement?" she smiled as they pulled apart after a long time.

"No way!" said Ross. "Will you marry me when we're out of this?"

"Sure, honey," she drawled, and they kissed again - long, lingering, probing...

"Hey, you two! This is a fine time to be doing that." A young man, in U.S. naval officer's uniform, approached. "Don't you want to get off this old tub?"

They smiled and followed him, arm in arm, down the companionway and along to where the gangway had been lowered.

They looked down on the launches at the foot of the gangway.

"You two get in that one," said the officer, pointing to the launch in which Ian, Hallin and other members of the crew were sitting anxiously, watched by two armed sailors. Other launches were already ferrying the former prisoners towards the warship. They seemed to be concealing their jubilation successfully, Ross noted.

As their own launch drew away and set off in pursuit, Ross and Bobbie held on to each other as they gazed silently back at the *Duke of Argyll*, her sides mottled with rust that had not been visible from on board.

Back on the *Duke*, an officer and several sailors were completing their search to make sure no-one was left anywhere.

As they prepared to descend to the last remaining launch, the officer caught one of the men on the shoulder.

"What you got there, Wysebaum?"

"Souvenir, sir." The sailor proudly held up a navy blue three-cornered hat with white beading round the edge. "Found it on the hatch cover, sir."